Between

the

Lies

For Katie and Danny,
with love and thanks

A special thank you to Vassilios
for his help and advice

Kelpies is an imprint of Floris Books
First published in 2017 by Floris Books
© 2017 Cathy MacPhail

Cathy MacPhail has asserted her right under the
Copyright, Designs and Patent Act 1988 to be
identified as the Author of this work

This publisher acknowledges subsidy from
Creative Scotland towards the publication
of this volume

 Also available as an eBook

British Library CIP data available
ISBN 978-178250-352-1
Printed in Poland

Between the Lies

CATHY MACPHAIL

KELPIESEDGE

How long have I been here? I've lost track of time.

Nobody's coming. Nobody knows where I am.

Why was I so stupid? Please... somebody help me.

I've been screaming so loud my throat hurts and still nobody hears me. I'm afraid to scream now. Because it's even darker, and what if... what if the person who comes is *that* person.

I'm trying not to panic.

But what if nobody ever finds me?

Can't think like that or I'll go mad.

No, I will be saved. Hold onto that thought.

Someone will find me.

Someone has to.

ONE

 Greater Glasgow Police

Appeal for Information: Missing Teen – Port Glasgow area

Police Scotland are appealing for information to help trace a fourteen-year-old girl. Judith Tremayne is missing from her home in Port Glasgow. She was last seen on Friday around 18.00.

Judith is described as tall for her age, with long brown hair and brown eyes. She was last seen wearing a green jacket, a t-shirt and blue jeans. Her parents have said it is completely out of character for Judith not to be in contact with them or her friends. Officers are becoming increasingly concerned for her welfare.

Anyone with information please contact the Greenock police station immediately.

247 📧 168 ♡ 71 ○

Greater Glasgow Police

Appeal for Information: Missing Teen...

---

andreaglass15 shared **Greater Glasgow Police**'s post

If anyone has any information about my bestezt friend, Jude, please can you come forward. Anything at all. Please share this post. We have to find her.

27 ⬛ 8♥ 9💬

---

xtraceymullanx shared **andreaglass15**'s post

Jude if you're reading this, please get in touch.

14 ⬛ 6♥ 2💬

---

belindab25 commented:

Everybody is worried sick about you.

0♥

And that was how it all began, with Judith being reported missing. Our school, St Thomas High, was buzzing with the news on the Monday. Groups gathering in the corridors, girls gossiping in the toilets, everyone sharing everything online.

The same photo peered out of everyone's posts: Jude, with her long hair draped over her shoulders, her big eyes wide, her mouth open as if she was just about to catch a fish. Bet she would hate that photo, I thought. Jude Tremayne was vain. Always liked to look her best. And that definitely wasn't her best shot.

Everyone was speculating about why she had gone.

"I heard she had a fight with her parents."

"She was always fighting with them," Andrea, her so-called 'bestezt' friend, admitted through tears. "They're a weird couple. All they ever want to do is trek through the wild. And camp. They were always dragging Jude off somewhere she didn't want to go."

"Maybe that's why she ran away. Maybe she hitched a lift to Benidorm."

Everyone laughed. Even Andrea. Though she tried to look guilty about it.

The chat went from drama to comedy as quickly as that, then back to drama.

"Maybe she didn't hitch a lift. She might have been snatched. There's a lot of creepy people about. If she walked along the waterfront at the port, no one could see from the street. Anybody could have got her." I thought I heard a little bit of hope in Tracey

Mullan's voice. Tracey was another so-called best friend of Jude's. She had a pale voice to match her pale face and hair. I always thought she looked as if the colour had been drained out of her.

"She's only been gone a couple of days. They'll probably find her holed up with her auntie in Glasgow, watching all the attention she's getting on the news."

Andrea tried to stifle a giggle. I could tell she didn't want anyone to think she saw the funny side of this. "That's a terrible thing to say, as if she would do anything like that."

"Jude's not a cruel person," Big Belinda Brown agreed. She always agreed with Andrea. She shook her head. "No, I'm with Tracey. I think she's been snatched." She said it as if it was the worst possible scenario, but definitely the one she'd enjoy the most.

"No," Andrea said. "She'll come back."

We all knew if Jude didn't come back it would only get worse (or better, depending on your point of view).

I didn't take part in the conversation, only listened, standing apart from the rest in the corridor outside the toilets. I was always apart from the rest; nobody wanted Abbie Kerr to be part of their group.

Jude was no particular friend of mine, after all. I had no particular friends in this school. My dad and I only moved here a few months ago when he got a job at Greenock. Before that, we lived in Glasgow. Mind you, I hadn't had many friends at my Glasgow school either. No-mates-Abbie. That was me.

But I listened with interest.

Jude didn't come back. According to the news, she was spotted everywhere.

Missing girl seen on Aberdeen Megabus →

Girl matching Judith Tremayne's description seen on London train →

Has Jude Tremayne joined ISIS? Glasgow teen may have gone to Syria →

That week it was all we talked about.

"Would she really run away because of a fight with her parents?" I asked some of the girls in class.

"She's a drama queen," I was told. "Judith Tremayne would turn burnt toast into a drama."

"She was always looking for attention," someone else said.

"Well, maybe she's doing it to get her parents' attention. Maybe she feels they've been neglecting her."

I looked at the girl who said that. Frances Delaney. Older than me by a couple of years, she was one of those girls that other girls seem to flock around, follow, copy. They all wanted to be like her.

She came in one day with a designer bag hung on her elbow, and the next day almost every girl was carrying a designer bag around. Frances had fair hair that always looked tousled. She'd pin it up on top of her head, but strands of it would hang untidily on her shoulders. You could sit for hours aiming to get your hair like Frances's, but you'd still never manage it. I know; I've tried. Yes, even me, Abbie Kerr, the outsider. The day I came in with my black hair tousled, thinking I looked exactly like a black-haired double of Frances, someone told me I had a bed head, and should get out my brush and fix it. Never did that again.

Frances always wore high heels. You heard her coming before you saw her, clattering along the corridors or up the winding steel stairs to the top floor. Other girls tried to copy that too. But have you ever tried to walk in high heels? Everyone either toppled over, or tripped up. It was comical to watch. And they got told not to wear high heels to school. But Frances seemed to walk in her heels with ease and somehow avoided being told off.

Frances waved her hands around as she talked about Jude. Her long fingers and almond-shaped nails fascinated me. "She wants her mum and dad to miss her, so when she comes back they'll welcome her with open arms and apologise, even though they haven't done anything wrong." She held out her arms as if she was welcoming a child: "Oh darlink, come to Mamma." Her accent became foreign. "I vill never take you camping again!" And she clutched an imaginary Jude to her bosom.

"I thought you liked her, Frances," I said.

She looked surprised. "I do, actually. She's harmless. She can be a bit silly, though, and easily led."

Someone called out, "Put it this way, she's not the brightest bulb on the Christmas tree."

Everyone laughed.

Frances went on. "You can like someone and still see their faults. I like everybody. Don't I, girls?"

And all her coven of friends laughed and agreed with her.

Actually, the truth was that everybody liked Frances. I'd never heard anyone say a bad word about her.

"Bet she doesn't like me," I said in a whisper, but it turned out the boy standing beside me, Robbie Grant, was close enough to hear.

"Does anybody?"

"Thanks for that, Robbie." Robbie never failed to get my back up. We should have got along: we were both loners, always in some kind of trouble.

He shrugged. "You've never fallen under the Frances spell, or hung on her every word, like they do."

He nodded across to where Frances seemed to be leading her friends down the corridor like the *Queen Mary* sailing off followed by a flotilla of small boats.

Maybe Robbie was right. I had never been interested in following anyone. Nor did I want to be a leader. I just wanted to be me. A loner. That was my problem. I didn't even have a best friend. But I did like watching things from a distance: the observer, watching and listening. And Judith's disappearance was the most interesting thing that had happened in yonks.

TWO

After almost a week, she hadn't come back.

Her parents were on the news every night pleading for her return. I watched her tearful mother, holding a handkerchief to her face, her hand held by a comforting policewoman. Not by her husband, Jude's dad. Was that because she blamed him for Judith running away? That's what I mean about observing. I wondered how many other people had noticed that.

Not many at St Thomas High anyway. And I could see their sympathy turn away from Jude.

"How could she do this to her mum and dad?"

"Did you see them on tv last night? They looked devastated."

"She'd better come back."

A police news conference with the Tremaynes

was shown on every screen in our school. There's a big screen in the atrium where the school cafe is. We have all our breaks there. And there are screens in the break-out zones on each of the three floors of the school, plus some in hallways too, like where you come in the front doors. At St Thomas High, we have our own television studio to broadcast from, which goes online by linking to the school website and it can even stream BBC news. It's run by the older kids, though Robbie, in my year, helps there too, because he's an I.T. clever clogs.

So the news was everywhere, and attitudes were changing about Jude. You could tell by the comments online.

Princess4581 commented:

How can she do this to her parents?

62 ♡

WeePal23 commented:

That's cruel.

34 ♡

Only Andrea stuck up for her.

> That's cruel.

andreaglass15 commented:
If she hasn't come back there must be a good reason. Jude would never do anything like this.
8 ♥

There were tears emojis in every one of Andrea's posts. Made me laugh really. Suddenly Jude was her 'bestezt' friend again, when only weeks ago she had drummed her out of their gang. I had been the one who found Jude in the toilets, crying harder than any emoji. I'd wanted to do a quick about-turn when I saw her, but, for some reason I will never fathom, she began to pour her heart out to me.

Of course I told her she was making a complete fool of herself, crying over Andrea Glass. I certainly wouldn't cry over losing somebody like that.

"But you've not got any friends to lose anyway," Jude said. That made me laugh. There am I trying to comfort her and she insults me.

"Even if I did, nothing and nobody would make me crack up like you, I would never let anybody get to me like that. It makes you look like a real wimp. And for a boring loser like Andrea? Grow a backbone, Jude, I'd never let anyone break me like that."

I was only trying to make her feel better, build up her self-esteem, but it made her cry even harder. I realised then that I wasn't a natural comforter, and I made a quick getaway. I suppose, looking back, she *was* being a bit of a drama queen.

So Andrea's tears emojis looked pretty flakey to me, knowing how upset she'd made Jude back then. And they weren't making people sad for Jude now. I could tell, if Jude didn't come back soon, everybody would turn against her.

I was in English when I got the message. Felt my phone vibrate in my pocket. Mr Madden, our English teacher, threw me one of his threatening looks, warning me not to check it. With a lot of teachers I would just ignore that look, take out my phone and read the message anyway. Half the class would do the same; a lot of them sit on their phones in lessons. But nobody did that with Mr Madden.

I wasn't really that interested anyway. I knew who it would be. My dad. Probably to tell me he'd be late in, working late or at another union meeting. Who else would message me? It certainly wouldn't be a friend. Ha! I say 'friend' in the loosest possible way.

Even when my phone buzzed again, with a 'Hey, you've got a message, pal, are you going to look at me or what?' sound – scolding me – I was still in no real hurry.

I only took it out of my pocket as I left the classroom. I read the message and stopped dead in the corridor.

It was from Judith Tremayne.

> **Jude**
> I want to come home

THREE

I'm not a screamy kind of girl, or a drama queen. Not my style. So, for a moment, I did nothing. Just stood there, thinking. I knew, later, they would all ask me what was going through my head. They would ask why Judith Tremayne would be messaging me.

I walked into the toilets. It was break and there were girls fixing their hair, washing their hands, gossiping. Tracey Mullan turned to look at me. "What's wrong with you?"

Did I look pale? I wondered. Or pal*er*. (My natural skin tone is peely-wally.) I held out the phone. "I've had a message." I took a deep breath. "From Jude."

"What!" Tracey yelled the word out, and snatched the phone from me. She stared into the screen with most of the girls crowding in behind her to see too. "It says: *I want to come home!*" Tracey shouted out, as if no one else could read.

Andrea Glass came flying out of one of the cubicles. I hadn't even realised anyone was in there. She grabbed the phone from Tracey. She read the message, then she glared at me. "How come Jude's messaging you? You were no special friend of hers. You're no special friend of anybody's!" She turned to the others for support. "I mean, everyone knows Jude was *my* best friend."

"You dumped her, Andrea," I reminded her. Everyone knew about their big argument.

She took a step towards me. Her dark curly hair seemed to quiver with her anger. I thought she was ready to jump me.

It was Tracey who stepped in. "Does it really matter who she got in touch with, Andrea? At least we know she's alive."

But Andrea had asked a very good question. Why would Jude choose me? I knew they would all be wondering that.

Then everything happened fast. I was almost frogmarched to the head's office, where Mr Barr immediately contacted the police. "Have you tried calling her back, Abbie?" he asked while we waited.

I always find it hard not to stare at Mr Barr. His head looks as if it's melted into his neck in folds. All he needs is a wick on top to look like a candle.

"Yes, sir, but her phone seems to be turned off or out of range: the message I sent says

✓ Sent
✓ Not Delivered"

It made sense really that my message couldn't be delivered. I knew just about everyone in the school had been calling Jude's number on a regular basis, longing to be the one whose call would be answered. The phone was either dead, or just rang out.

"And why would Jude text you?" The question I was dreading. So I asked a question of my own.

"She wants to come home... So what's stopping her? Does it mean she's in danger or something?"

"Not necessarily," Mr Barr said, trying to comfort me, as if I needed comforting. I wasn't worried about Jude. Couldn't tell him that, of course. "Jude could be worried about coming back, facing the music. She might think she's in some kind of trouble. Wants to come back, but is afraid of what she might face when she does."

When the police arrived an hour later, they said

the same thing. They also wanted me to try again to reply.

"Tell her everyone wants her home. She's not in any trouble."

So I typed that into my phone and sent it. Then I held it out to the policeman. "It can't deliver it. The message hasn't arrived."

As I walked back to class, everyone wanted to know if I'd heard any more from Jude. I told them I'd sent her the reply telling her everyone wants her home. Got to the point I was fed up repeating it. I looked up at the big screen in the upper corridor and an idea came to me. If I could send a message round the whole school I wouldn't have to keep repeating myself. So I didn't go to class. I made my way to the television studio on the second floor. It's just a classroom that's been set up with cameras and sound equipment, but we give it the grand name of 'the studio'. I remember Andrea being pissed off because Robbie was allowed to work there but not her. "I'm better at I.T. than you are, ask anybody."

And his answer had made me smile. "You're the apprentice, hen. I'm the master."

I knocked on the door and to my surprise it was Robbie himself who opened it. I hadn't expected him to be there during class time.

"What are you doing here?" We both asked it at once.

"I'm a trainee cameraman," he said smugly.

"Hope they've got the cameras chained to the wall then."

"And to what do we owe the honour of a visit from you."

I pushed past him. "I want to speak to someone in charge."

Fifth years were in charge of the studio and one of them suddenly appeared from behind a large monitor. I'd seen him around the school but didn't know his name. I told him what I wanted.

Robbie sniggered behind him when he heard me. "She wants to broadcast to the school. Ha!"

But he shut up quick when the fifth year, who introduced himself as Angus Watt, didn't laugh. "That's a good idea, Abbie," he said. "This is ok with Mr Barr?"

"Oh yeah," I lied.

He nodded towards a stool. "Sit down. If you're ready we can do it now, and play it on a loop."

"On a loop?" I asked.

"Just means we play it over and over."

"Oh flip, her face on a big screen? It's not Halloween already, is it?"

"Oh come on, Robbie, Abbie's very pretty."

No one ever said that about me, except my mother a long time ago. I blushed, and I never do that. It gave Robbie a good excuse for another snipe. "Would madam require hair and make-up? A lot of make-up? In fact, I don't think we have that much."

But Angus put him in his place. "Get the camera set up, Robbie, or you are out of here."

Then he turned to me. "Ok Abbie, let's get this show on the road."

FOUR

I was sure that I wouldn't be able to talk, not in front of those cameras. And at first I did freeze, but once I had begun, it just came pouring out. I told them about the message, and speaking to Mr Barr and the police. I urged everyone watching to try to contact Jude.

"Did it go out live?" I asked Angus.

"Yeah," he said. "It goes out live."

"You're a natural, Abbie," Robbie said when I finished. He was being sarcastic. "But I can't figure why she messaged you, of all people."

I had come up with an even more logical answer to that.

"Maybe I'm just the first name on her speed dial. 'A' is for Abbie?"

Robbie shrugged. "Oh well, you've now made

your first step into stardom. It'll be 'I'm a Celebrity Get Me Out Of Here' next."

By the time I left the studio my face was on every screen in the school. My voice echoed from the glass ceiling to the floor. I was surprised by the reaction. And pleased.

"That was a great idea, Abbie."

"I wondered what that blinking studio was for; now I know."

And even, "You look terrific on screen."

Me, getting compliments?

And everywhere, people were messaging and posting. They were reaching out to Jude.

Wee_Weegie05

Come home Jude. We all love you.

207 🔁 128 ♡ 28 💬

---

invygirl_x commented:

Don't be afraid. Come home.

61 ♡

---

stars_xo commented:

Ur the best Jude.

32 ♡

But by the end of the day, no one had had a reply. And by the end of the day, I had had another idea.

When the bell rings, everyone floods out as if the school is on fire. They can't escape quick enough. That day, I hovered by the gates. I took off my school tie, and I tied it around the iron railings.

Someone behind me called out, "What are you doing?"

I looked back. It was one of the sixth-year boys. "It's for Jude!"

He laughed. And he whipped off his tie and fastened it beside mine. He shouted out to friends: "Where's your tie?"

Within minutes the gate was festooned, the ties flying like standards in the wind. Our school colours are maroon and yellow, and they looked really bright on that grey day.

I shouted out, "Take photos! Send them to Jude! Hashtag: ComeHomeJude." Seconds later all the phones were flashing.

Robbie came along. "Hey, what's happening here?"

I didn't even answer him. Daft question. It was obvious what was going on. A group of girls had started making a video of it all. My social media account was a long scroll of maroon-and-yellow-tie pics. **#ComeHomeJude**

Robbie hadn't expected an answer anyway. "You do realise these ties'll all get nicked overnight? They'll be on eBay by the morning."

"You have a very low opinion of everybody, Robbie."

"And you, Mother Teresa? You don't?"

I walked past him and bumped right into Andrea and company. I was expecting another insult, but instead I saw Andrea was taking her tie off too. She tried not to look at me, almost as if she was ashamed to be caught joining in. As her tie came off, so did Belinda's and Tracey's. They glared at me, defying me to say a word.

"Mr Barr'll be raging about this," Belinda said to nobody in particular. But she tied her tie on the railings anyway.

Dad wasn't home. Nothing unusual there. He sent me a text. He had another union meeting. So when the doorbell rang around seven, I thought it was him, home early for a change, and I opened the door without checking, something he was always warning me not to do. But it wasn't Dad. It was Jude's parents.

I had seen them once in the flesh, at a parents' meeting at the school. They looked the same on the front step as they had then. Matching Berghaus jackets and wellies. I remember Jude being mortified when they walked into the class.

Jude's mum just about fell through the doorway in her eagerness to get to me. She grabbed my shoulders. "Has she been in touch again? Did she say where she is?" She looked as if she'd been crying for days.

Her husband helped her to a chair. "I'm sorry, barging in like this. But we had to come. The police told us you had a message from Jude."

"Can I see the message?"

I handed them my phone and Mrs Tremayne read it over and over, and then she held the phone to her chest, as if she could feel the beating heart of her daughter through it. She was crying so hard I felt like crying too.

"I've not had any more messages. If I do, I'll contact you right away."

"At least we know she's all right," she said through her sobs. "*If* she is. She wants to come home… Why doesn't she then?"

I couldn't answer her. "I don't know," was all I said.

Mrs Tremayne was talking as if she needed to explain. "We'd had a silly argument, that was all. I don't even know how it started." She looked at her husband.

"It wasn't my fault, Ruth," he said, and it was clear it wasn't the first time he'd said it, and it wouldn't be the last.

Mrs Tremayne shook her head. "I know. I just wish we hadn't argued with her at all."

"We put it down to her age, her mood," Mr Tremayne went on, as if I deserved an explanation.

His wife leaned across and touched my hand. "I want to tell her, whatever we did, we're sorry. Can you send a message saying that to her?"

"I've tried sending messages. They're never delivered." But even as I spoke I was typing it in. I showed Mrs Tremayne. Under the message:

✓ Not Delivered

"Why did she send a message to you… and not us?"

"I don't know. I hardly talked to Jude at school."

Mr Tremayne sat on the arm of the chair, comforting his wife. "She thought we were too strict. Too many rules and regulations. We weren't fun like other parents. She thought we were the most boring parents in the world."

"But there was something else going on," Mrs Tremayne continued. "Something at the school. She was being secretive, always hiding her phone as if she was afraid we'd see something on it. Was she being bullied? Do you know, Abbie?"

It would have been the wrong time to point out that Jude ran with the crowd more likely to *do* the bullying.

"As a favour, Abbie," her dad asked, "please would you try to find out? Your friends are more likely to tell you than the police. You might uncover the reason she ran away."

He didn't want it to be their fault. He needed assurance it wasn't his fault.

I could only agree. "I'll do my best."

FIVE

I saw the television van as soon as the bus approached school next morning. There was a journalist, and a cameraman with his camera trained along the school gates. Everyone on the bus got excited.

"It's that Sara Flynn!" someone shouted. And they all surged towards the windows for a closer look.

Sara Flynn, the most high-profile news reporter on tv (well, at least in Scotland) was here at our school. Of course when the bus stopped, no one headed into the school building. They all made a beeline for the gates.

"This is wonderful!" Sara Flynn said. She was in full make-up on this blustery morning, her red hair perfect, not even moving in the wind. "Is Abbie Kerr here?"

I found myself being pushed to the front, though I struggled against it. Then I was facing the lovely Sara. "So I believe this was all your idea?" Her free hand waved along the line of ties on the railings.

I took a deep breath. "It's just to show Jude. Everyone sent photos to her, and uploaded them to all our accounts – the hashtag is ComeHomeJude. I thought if she saw this, she'd know how much we want her back."

"And you got a message from her too?"

"Yes."

The school bell rang. I was never so glad to hear it. I could feel myself beginning to sweat and I didn't want any more of her questions.

"Come on, Abbie," a voice called out. "Can we have a pic?" It was a photographer from the local paper.

Sara Flynn said, "You should be very proud of this, Abbie."

"The girl done good," someone shouted.

I smiled and a camera flashed.

Mr Barr came to speak to me almost as soon as I went inside. I was expecting him to go on at me about the ties on the gates. Instead he beamed at me. "You're getting us very good publicity, Abbie," he said. "I've had a call from that Sara Flynn complimenting me on the way the pupils are rallying around for Judith. She wants an interview later."

"You don't mind the ties, sir?"

He dismissed the very idea with a wave of his hand. "If the parents don't object, why should I? Hopefully it will only be for a day or two."

"Yes, a day or two," I agreed. "Would it be alright if I used the studio feed again, sir?"

I began to explain about the Tremaynes coming to my house, but it seemed I didn't need a reason or an excuse. "Of course, if it's going to help bring Judith back, what can I say? You're doing great, Abbie."

So during lunch break I went back to the studio. Unfortunately, Robbie was there too. "Ah, she has returned. The star of the show."

I brushed past him. "You're only allowed in here during lunch because you're barred from anywhere else in the school."

Angus was there too, having his lunch at one of the desks. "What do you want this time?"

"To tell the school what the police said."

"You got the ok from the police for that?"

"Yes. They're issuing a statement too."

That was a bit of a lie. I hadn't even asked them.

Robbie let out a snort of laughter. "Issuing a statement! You're getting better by the minute, Abbie."

Angus snapped at him, "Get the camera ready, Robbie."

So, once again, I was on the school news feed. I felt more at ease this time. Jude's parents had asked me to help: no one could fault me – I was only doing what they wanted. But I was glad Robbie was behind the camera and I couldn't see his face. I was sure he would be sniggering at me.

I began by telling them what the police had said. "The good news is they're sure Judith's not far. She's somewhere in the area. She wants to come home, but they don't think she's in any danger. The police think that she's scared to come home for some reason. And maybe one of us, someone in the school, knows why she really ran away, and why she might be afraid to come back." My mouth was drying up. I had to pause to take a breath. "Was anyone bullying her? Was she having trouble with anyone in school? If you have any idea, let me know. It will be completely confidential. Just remember: we have to help Judith. And keep using the hashtag: ComeHomeJude."

"Where did all that come from?" Robbie asked as soon as it was over. "She was being bullied? Judith Tremayne was being bullied?"

"I'm only saying what her parents said, what they think. I'm not making anything up."

Angus patted me on the back. "You'll get people talking, Abbie. You are your father's daughter."

My father's daughter. Dad was always on his high horse about something: marching or protesting or organising strikes. He hadn't made a lot of friends because of that.

Robbie waited till Angus was out of earshot before he whispered. "You're loving this, in't ye?"

"I'm just trying to help, right!"

"People are actually beginning to think you're awright. You're pretty cool. The wicked witch has turned into the fairy godmother, eh?" He leaned forward. "I don't think a leopard can change its spots, hen."

"I won't even answer that, Robbie, it's so clear you don't like me, but then, you don't like anybody, do you?" and I stormed away from him. I wouldn't let Robbie bother me.

But he did.

SIX

Big Belinda was waiting for me when I went downstairs. We call her Big Belinda because she's the tallest girl in the school and built like a sumo wrestler. I wouldn't like to meet her on a dark night… or get on the wrong side of her. And by the look on her red face when she saw me, the wrong side was exactly where I was.

"Jude was being bullied? Where did you hear that?"

I tried not to look as scared as I felt. "It was her parents who suggested that, not me."

"I hope you're not trying to imply it was me that was bullying her?"

"Guilty conscience, Belinda?" Because if anybody *was* bullying Jude, Big Belinda would be the chief suspect. She bullied just about everybody else in the school.

"Aye, well I better not be getting the blame for this. Or you'll be sorry."

Still, Angus was right. My broadcast had got everyone talking.

"She was being awful secretive about something," one of the girls told me.

"I saw her hiding her phone from me," another said. "I thought maybe she was getting abusive messages."

And then there were the posts and comments.

Gingernut72 commented:

Bullying is a terrible thing #ComeHomeJude

10 ♡

Laughandlove commented:

There was def something fishy going on with her.

5 ♡

Princess4581 commented:

Andrea fell out with her. Broke her heart.

0 ♡

Andrea somehow managed to see that one, and when she did, there really was trouble. She came rushing at me in the corridor. She looked furious. "What did you mean, do we know anything about Jude being bullied? Did you mean me?! I did not bully Jude – she was my friend – she's still my friend." With every word she was pushing at me.

I grabbed her hands and held her away. "If the shoe fits, Andrea..."

That sent her into a rage. "Me and Jude were ready to make up. Ask anybody."

That wasn't what I had heard, but I just shrugged. "Anything you say, Andrea."

And then suddenly the anger seemed to leave her. She was in tears. "Please don't say Jude and me falling out had anything to do with her running away. We fell out, that was all." She gripped my jacket as if she was afraid she would fall if she didn't. "I'm sorry, Abbie. What you said, it made me feel so guilty. And you're doing all this to find her, and I'm doing nothing. And I'm supposed to be her friend – I feel so bad." There were murmurs of sympathy round the group that had gathered to watch.

I could see, though, that she was embarrassing Tracey, who tried to pull her away. "Come on,

Andrea. You're showing yourself up."

But Andrea still clung to me. "If there's anything I can do to help, just ask. If she sends you another message... Tell her I'm sorry, will you, Abbie?"

Now she was embarrassing me. "I will, Andrea. I will."

Tracey got her away at last. She put her arms around her and led her off down the corridor, glaring back at me as they went.

Robbie stood with me and watched them. "You've moved Andrea Glass to tears. Never thought I'd see the day. I don't like her, you know," he added, as if I was interested. "She tried to get me chucked off the studio team."

"Pity she didn't succeed," I said, and walked away.

That night I was on the front of the local paper. My photo, my story.

ST THOMAS GIRL LEADS CAMPAIGN

"The girl done good!" say the school friends of Abbie Kerr, who has started a social media campaign to contact Judith Tremayne: #ComeHomeJude. Judith has been missing from home and school for over a week.

I hated seeing photos of myself usually. My face always looks too white, my hair too black: I really do look like a Goth. But this photo flattered me – the way I was turning to the camera and smiling. I never smile for a camera. Caught me unawares that one did. The school ties were waving behind me. It was a good article too. Giving me all the credit for the ties and the publicity about Jude. I even made the television. Sara Flynn, standing in the wind with hair like concrete, talking to me. Clips of it were shared everywhere online: **#ComeHomeJude**. Dad and I watched it and I could tell how proud he was.

"That's a great interview. You said all the right things, Abbie. That Jude should be glad to have you as her friend."

What he said made me want to cry. I always wanted to make him proud. Now here I was getting my wish, and all I could do was cry.

Next day, as soon as I walked into school, that photograph hit me in the face. There I was on the big screen in the atrium, twenty times real size, smiling down at everyone like some benevolent dictator.

"You look quite fit, Abbie," one of the boys

shouted, and some of the others started whistling and stamping their feet. I don't know how to handle compliments like that, so I marched straight off to class, blushing like mad.

Andrea was waiting for me at the door. I hoped she wasn't going to cry again. I couldn't handle that either. "The head's had me in his office, wanted to know if it was true that I had fallen out with Jude."

"I never mentioned your name, Andrea," I said quickly.

"No, I know that. It's because they're trying to find out why she ran away, and maybe why she's scared to come back. She might be scared to come back if she was being bullied, mightn't she?"

"I didn't say it was you, Andrea. Honest. I don't even think she was being bullied."

A crowd had gathered round us. Listening to our every word. Probably hoping for a bit of grievous bodily harm.

"You and Jude used to be best mates, Andrea," one of the girls said.

Yeah, Andrea, Jude, Tracey and Big Belinda, always together. And making a point of keeping me out of their precious little circle. Then, just a few weeks ago, Jude was pushed out too.

"Maybe that's why she didn't text you, Andrea."

There was a murmur of agreement.

Andrea swung round to face the crowd. But her eyes had filled with tears again. "Ok, we fell out. I feel bad enough about that. But mates do fall out, don't they? Jude and I were going to be friends again."

I don't think any of them believed that. I was sure I could read the doubt in their faces.

Then Andrea suddenly stood up straight. It was as if someone had shoved a steel rod up her back. "Yes, I put my hand up: we fell out. And I wish I could let her know how sorry I am about that, but it wasn't me she was scared of... Was it, Belinda?" She shook her head as if she couldn't bear to say anything else, and then pushed through the crowd around us to get away.

Big Belinda was right in front of me. She always stood too close: invading your space, I think they call it. We were all waiting for her to tell us what Andrea meant. "I think it's a sin, blaming Andrea." She poked me in the chest with a fat chip finger. "If you're looking for somebody Jude was scared of, check out that creepy old man who lives in her street. He's weird – Jude always said he was weird. Creepy Creen she used to call him. If she was scared of anybody, it was him."

SEVEN

I hated having to see Jude's mum and dad. Their pain was so obvious I could hardly bear to watch them. There were photographs of them in the paper, their faces drawn and tear-stained.

It was that article in the local paper that brought Mr and Mrs Tremayne back to my house. "We had to come and say thank you… for everything." Mrs Tremayne hugged me. I'm not a hugging type of person and I cringed, but she didn't seem to notice. "We heard about you asking if anyone was bullying her."

"I don't know if it will help. No one will admit to bullying her of course, but she was so hurt when Andrea dumped her." Should I have said that? It just came out.

Mrs Tremayne's face darkened. "That girl. I think she was a bad influence. Judith is easily led, you know. And then to drop her the way she did. That hurt Jude so much."

"Andrea said they were ready to be friends again?" I made it sound more like a question.

Mrs Tremayne tutted. "I don't believe that. I saw no sign of it... Though Jude was phoning someone, wasn't she?" she turned to her husband and he nodded.

"Yes, she seemed very secretive about it," he said. "Maybe it was this Andrea, I don't know. Did you hear anything else, Abbie?"

I held back for a moment. Should I tell them what Belinda had told me? I was wary of getting someone into trouble, but how could I keep quiet? "Someone..." I wouldn't say who, "Someone said there was a creepy old man on your street she was a bit scared of?"

They looked at each other then back at me. "On our street? I can't think of—"

Mrs Tremayne broke in: "She couldn't mean Mr Creen?"

"Yes," I said at once. "Creepy Creen, that's what she called him."

"He's quiet, lives alone, keeps himself to himself... But Jude never said a word to us about him!"

Mr Tremayne's face lost all colour. "She'd be scared to. Would we have believed her?"

Mrs Tremayne seemed to sag. "Oh my... I thought she'd run away, but if... someone... took her... If someone hurt her..." She sank into a chair. "We have to tell the police about this."

I had a terrible feeling Mr Tremayne was about to hug me now.

I stepped back.

"You see, this is what I mean, Abbie. Jude's friends would never tell the police about this. Thank you, Abbie. Please keep doing what you're doing. You're finding out more than the police have."

I cried when they left. "Our girl will come home," I heard them whisper to each other as they walked, hands held tight, down our path. Jude had always said they were cold and heartless. Well, if they had been like that before, they certainly weren't now.

I was still crying when my dad came in. "You're taking this too hard, Abbie."

"I wish she hadn't sent me that message." And I meant it. "I wish I wasn't involved in all this."

"Well she did. And you're doing great. You're taking charge." I knew he would approve of that.

Everyone seemed to be approving of me. I was drowning in messages.

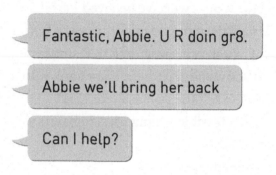

Fantastic, Abbie. U R doin gr8.

Abbie we'll bring her back

Can I help?

And on and on. I had never had so much attention, so many compliments. People smiling in corridors, patting me on the back as I passed them. Praising me. I had never had so much admiration. Did I like it? Yes, more than I would ever have imagined.

The next night Andrea phoned me.

I was wary of answering her call at first. Why was she phoning me? I didn't want her crying again.

"Abbie, I'm sorry about today. If Jude and me hadn't fallen out, maybe she wouldn't have run away. Maybe it is my fault." She stumbled over the words as if there was a lump in her throat. "But I'm not as heartless as you think, Abbie. All Jude would go on about was her mum and dad and how much she hated them... She wasn't interested in any of my life, what was going on for me. I wanted to talk about some stuff at home, and she hardly listened. And I lost it with her. That's how we fell out. I told her she was the most selfish person I had ever met."

That sounded just like the Jude I knew. "I'm sorry to hear that, Andrea, that must have been awful."

There was still a sob in her voice when she answered me. "It was... It still is, Abbie. Anyway, I just wanted to say, keep doing what you're doing. It's brought the whole school together. Everybody thinks you're fantastic. I never thought you could be like this. I never liked you, to be honest, but you've been a revelation."

She hardly let me get a word in. I wouldn't have known what to say if she had. Everybody thinks I'm fantastic? Andrea Glass complimenting me?

Keep doing what you're doing. Jude's parents had told me that too. So I would. I hadn't any choice. I was in too deep now. And I had already decided what I would do next.

EIGHT

Next day I was in front of the cameras again. Robbie couldn't say a word, though his sneer when I walked into the studio spoke volumes. But for now I was the darling of the school. When I'd asked Mr Barr for permission he'd agreed immediately. "You're doing wonders for our reputation, Abbie."

ST THOMAS'S UNITED SCHOOL COMES TOGETHER IN SEARCH FOR MISSING GIRL

That was the headline in one of the Glasgow papers yesterday, and there was a photo of Mr Barr standing against a background of waving ties.

"So, Abbie, what is it this time?" Angus asked.

But I wouldn't tell him. I wanted the whole school to hear this together.

First, I thanked everyone for their help. "Don't just give me praise," I told them. "We're all in this together." And I brought them up to date with everything (though I didn't mention Creepy Creen). "Jude's mum and dad are so grateful for what we're doing and they want us to keep up the momentum. Jude has to be out there, maybe listening, maybe watching." I took a deep breath. "So, I suggest we have a candlelit vigil tonight at Jude's house. Let's all gather there around six, let's light up the skies for Judith."

As soon as the camera stopped rolling, Robbie laughed at me. "Where did that come from? A candlelit blinkin' vigil?"

"I think it's a nice idea. It'll let Jude know we all care about her, and Mr and Mrs Tremayne want me to keep on helping," my voice was rising with every word, "and what harm will it do anyway?!" I could feel my eyes well up with tears and I hated myself for that. "Why don't you ever think I'm sincere about anything?"

Robbie stepped back, still with his eyebrows raised. "Wow! They look almost like real tears."

I sniffed them back and rubbed at my eyes. "They are. No matter what you think." And they were. I promised myself they were.

I pushed away from him only to career into Mr Madden, who was coming into the studio. "Why are you crying, Abbie?" he looked beyond me to Robbie. "Are you responsible for this?" He didn't wait for an answer. He took me by the elbow and led me away. "I think it's wonderful what you're doing, Abbie. The teachers will be at your candlelit vigil tonight too."

I hadn't expected that. Wasn't sure that I wanted it. But I had no power to stop it. I had set the snowball rolling, and now nothing was going to slow it down.

All afternoon the vigil was what everyone talked about. The word was spread with messages and posting everywhere.

---

abbiekerr

Vigil tonight, for Judith, outside the Tremaynes' house, 6pm. Bring candles. #ComeHomeJude

334 🎬 485 ❤ 54 💬

Social_Butterflii commented:

A candlelit #Vigil that will be so cool

176 ♡

MizzUnderstood commented:

Can you believe Abbie Kerr came up with that?

19 ♡

Glasgow_Grl commented:

I never liked her, but now... She's changed.

17 ♡

Mon_the_Morton commented:

That's what I think. She's been brilliant.

28 ♡

---

portybhoy88 commented:

See you tonight!

49 ♡

Only Belinda wasn't happy about it. "A candlelit vigil? I mean, who do you think you are? Organising everything."

"There was nothing to stop you from organising anything..." I tapped my teeth with my finger. "Oh, wait a minute. You're thick as a brick – you couldn't organise a prayer group in a convent."

How did I dare say that to Big Belinda? She looked ready to explode. She didn't have the brains to snap back a smart reply. I was saved from annihilation by the arrival of the majestic Frances Delaney.

"Hey, what's going on here?"

The light was behind her, illuminating her tousled blonde hair. She looked like some kind of superhero come to my rescue.

"Nothin' Frances," Belinda mumbled, and she stepped away from me. "We're just having a wee difference of opinion."

Frances ignored her. Her smile landed on me. "Great idea about the vigil, Abbie." She cast a glance at Belinda. "You'll be there, won't you, Belinda?"

"Sure will, Frances," Belinda must have hated having to say that. "Try and keep me away."

Frances linked her arm in mine. "So Abbie, do we have to bring our own candles?" Her laugh rang out and seemed to echo all through the school.

Mrs Tremayne called me just as school finished. Someone must have phoned her about it. "What a wonderful idea, Abbie. The neighbours are going to be there too, and people from the streets all around. Some of Jude's aunts and uncles are coming. And the paper's been in touch: they're sending a reporter and photographer. And the tv people are coming. That Sara Flynn. So much good publicity. Thank you so much."

More publicity than I had ever expected. I began to feel nervous.

NINE

I didn't want to go that night. I wasn't used to all this attention, I felt guilty and embarrassed and, if I could have, I would have stayed home. Dad couldn't even come with me; an important union meeting trumped my candlelit vigil.

"But I'll come along as soon as it finishes," he promised.

So I had to go alone. I had no choice. It was me who had organised it. Face the music, Abbie, I told myself. It will be over soon. A couple of hours and it will all be over.

It was such a perfect night for a candlelit vigil. Crisp and clear with not a cloud to hide the stars. I hadn't believed so many people would turn up. I expected the pupils from St Tom's to be there, maybe a couple of the neighbours Mrs Tremayne had referred to, but nothing like the massive crowd that was standing outside Jude's house when I arrived. I really did gasp, and I thought that was something people only did in books. There were pupils not only from our school but from some of the others in the town; people had come from neighbourhoods all around, and as far as I could tell, everyone from Jude's family was there too. They stretched all along the street and spilled onto the road. Some were standing in other people's gardens. They lined the walkway by the river on the other side of the street. It looked as if hundreds were there, maybe thousands. I spotted Mr Madden and some of the other teachers. He raised his hand in a wave when he saw me. A path was made for me as I walked through the crowd, like I was someone special, and when Mrs Tremayne spotted me, her eyes seemed to light up. She broke away from her husband and hurried towards me.

"Here she is. Here's the girl we owe for all this." She grabbed my arm and pulled me up the path to their front door. "The heroine of the hour: Abbie Kerr. No one's doing more than Abbie to help us find Judith."

And they all began to applaud me. Applaud me! I felt embarrassed, and guilty. I wanted to say: Not just me... please, I don't deserve this.

There was a shout from the crowd, then a cheer. Some of my schoolmates applauded too. Belinda had a sour look, as if she'd been eating something nasty, but Tracey and Andrea were clapping along with the rest. Boys let out loud whistles. I spotted Robbie whistling with the rest of them, and when he saw me he gave me the thumbs up. Did he mean it? Was he being sarcastic again?

"I wouldn't let them light the candles till you came, Abbie," Mrs Tremayne shouted over the crowd. "Do you think everybody's here now?" How could anyone else be coming? There was no room for anyone else. Even more had come since I arrived. "What do you think, Abbie?"

I looked at my watch, and round the crowds, and I nodded. "Ok," I said. I'd never felt so nervous.

"You first, Abbie."

I took my candle from my pocket and my hand shook as I held it over the match.

And then, after mine, all the candles were lit, one by one, and the street was illuminated with the glow from hundreds of candles. The air was icy cold, and the moon seemed huge hanging above us. There wasn't a breath of wind, so the flames hardly flickered. It was as if their glow spread out over the dark river and the lights across the water seemed to be lit for Jude too, joining in with us. It was breathtaking. All these people, here, for Jude. For a girl they hardly knew or hardly liked, praying for her safe return. I had to hold the tears in. I lifted my candle high. "This is for you, Jude, to show how much we want you back."

And every candle was raised and everyone shouted, "For Judith!"

Portyyy

Candle for you, Judith #ComeHomeJude

24 📧 46 🤍 12 ⭕

Sk8rboi

Check out all of us at the vigil

83 📧 121 🤍 74 ⭕

Mrs Tremayne leaned closer to me. "Are you crying, Abbie?" By then, I couldn't stop the tears from falling down my cheeks. Her arm went round me. "My, you're shaking." She squeezed me closer. "You've been such a good friend to us."

I had to hold back a sob. Mrs Tremayne was

crying too. She was nice woman. She didn't deserve this. What was Judith thinking about? But I had to draw in that sob. "Take a photo!" I called out. "Send it to her phone. I'll do it too. Let her see how much we want her to come back."

And now the sky was lit up with flashes from phones, including mine. I typed in a message:

Abbie
Time to come home Jude

And I prayed she would get it.

There was a roar on the road as a van drew up; the legend on the side read: **Scottish News**. The back doors opened and Sara Flynn stepped out, with her cameraman behind her. She pushed her way into the Tremayne's garden. Before we could really take in what she was doing, she turned to the camera and began to address it.

"We're here at the home of Jack and Ruth Tremayne, where so many of their friends and neighbours, including their daughter's school friends, have gathered to hold a candlelit vigil for the safe return of Judith." She turned to Mrs Tremayne. "How are you holding up?"

"All this is heartwarming for us. It's keeping my spirits up and my hopes that I will see my girl soon. But this girl," I tried to move away, but she drew me in closer to her, "this girl, Abbie, is the one responsible for all you see."

I wanted to melt into the crowd but Sara Flynn had me cornered. She smiled with her so-red lips. "Abbie. Abbie Kerr again, the heroine of the hour? You must be delighted with this turnout."

I tried to stop her from saying anything else. "Nothing to do with me really."

"Of course it is," Mrs Tremayne insisted. "She suggested the candlelit vigil. She went onto the school news channel and asked everyone to come." She laughed. "She'll be having your job soon, Ms Flynn."

"I only suggested it," my voice shook. I pointed into the crowd, all the faces glowed in the candlelight. "They came here for Judith. They should be getting the credit."

"And why do you think they came here, Abbie?"

It only took me a moment to give her an answer. I'd had this speech ready for ages. "Teenagers are never given credit for anything. We're always on computers, we're rude, we're selfish, we talk back to our parents, we don't care about anything.

Everyone thinks teenagers are lazy, and we don't obey the rules. But this is us," I spread my arms out towards the crowd, "the real us. We're teenagers but when something bad happens to one of us, we come together, we do the right thing and you see how much we care."

There was a sudden rousing cheer.

"Good for you, Abbie!"

"You tell 'em."

gordy44

Teens care. #ComeHomeJude

48 🔁 62 ❤ 27 💬

MizzUnderstood

Abbie says do the right thing #ComeHomeJude

32 🔁 49 ❤ 18 💬

Sara Flynn didn't stop smiling. "That was a wonderful little speech, Abbie." Was she being as sarcastic as Robbie? "Have you had any more texts from Judith?"

I looked out beyond the crowd, hardly listening to her now. I shook my head.

"Do you think this will bring her back?"

I do, I wanted to say. I *know* it will bring her back.

TEN

I looked around at all the candles, flames quivering now in the slight breeze that had risen up from the water. Magical. It looked magical. It was a magical moment: the perfect moment.

Come on, Jude.

Now was the time. The perfect time. Sara Flynn was there with her camera, all the pupils were waiting, the neighbours, the candlelight, Judith's mum and dad. Now was the time. I looked at my watch.

"Have you somewhere to go, Abbie?" Mrs Tremayne didn't wait for my answer. "It is cold. I think everyone's been here long enough." She began to call out to the crowd: "Thank you all for coming."

But I didn't want them to go, not then. I glanced again at my watch. "No, no, let them stay." Did I snap at her? "Mrs Tremayne, let's stay a little longer."

She put her arm round my shoulder and squeezed. "I think you can call me Ruth." And then I was almost crying again. She was a kind woman.

"Well, I think we have all we need here," Sara Flynn turned to her cameraman. "Let's go! I want to make the ten o'clock bulletin."

So did I, but she couldn't go now. "NO!" I said it too quickly. I touched her arm. "Just a bit longer."

Her face creased in a puzzled frown. "Why?"

Just a feeling, I wanted to say, but I didn't. "We can wait a bit longer, can't we?"

But the wind was rising, bitter and cold, and already candles were being extinguished, people beginning to drift off. I wanted them to stay. They had to stay. I checked my watch again. Then my phone.

"Why do you keep looking at the time, Abbie?" Sara Flynn suddenly didn't sound soft and friendly. She sounded suspicious. "Why are you so anxious for us to stay?"

"I think Jude deserves a little more time, that's all."

Jude's dad looks puzzled. "Abbie? Is something wrong?"

I looked along the street. People were moving away; the moment would soon be gone. I shook my head. I wanted to shout out to them to stay. "No. Nothing. Honest."

I didn't sound honest at all. I sounded guilty. As if I was hiding something.

"Are you expecting Jude to show up?"

I should have said yes right then. Said that I'd wondered whether she might have heard about the vigil and I thought she was going to walk towards us, among the candles, like something out of a movie. Or tell them she had messaged me today to say she was coming back. Or tell them I'd had a psychic moment and knew she was coming. But all I could do was check my phone again. "No. I mean, I don't know."

Too late.

There was hardly anyone left.

Something had gone wrong.

I wanted away too, but Sara Flynn wouldn't let me. She held me by the arm. "What makes you think she's going to show up tonight?"

"I didn't. I don't."

"Something's going on here, Abbie. Why do you keep looking at your phone?"

I wanted to push past her.

There were only a few stragglers left on the street. It would be pointless now. Pointless!

"What did you think was going to happen tonight? Were you expecting Judith to come back? What made you think that, Abbie? Is there something you're not telling us?" Question after question with hardly a second to answer, or to think.

If she'd given me that second, I could have covered it. Said Jude had messaged me, and that I wasn't to tell her parents. Or pretend that I thought I had seen her. Anything. Instead, I felt too guilty. I looked too guilty. I had had enough of this. It was all too much. It was meant to be over.

"Something is going on here, Abbie." Sara Flynn wasn't going anywhere now. She saw another story. The camera pushed in my face. I couldn't think straight. She was getting me all mixed up and puzzled and Jude was meant to be here by now and I couldn't take it any longer.

"She was supposed to come. Ok! She was supposed to walk down that street while all the candles were lit and the cameras were here and all the people. She was supposed to make an entrance!" The camera was running. And still I didn't stop talking. "That was the plan. She was to come back tonight."

ELEVEN

It was as if the sound was turned off. There was a silence. Everyone was looking at me. It seemed a long time without anyone reacting to what I said. I half hoped I had said it inside myself, that no one had heard me.

And then sound exploded around me. Everyone talked at once.

Sara Flynn's voice above them all, sharp and loud: "Abbie, what plan?"

The camera shoved closer.

And Jude's mum too. "She was supposed to come? What do you mean by that?"

But she didn't have to ask. Sara Flynn was figuring it all out by herself. "Are you saying you and Judith Tremayne came up with this together? That this has all been a hoax?"

I was shaking my head, trying to move past her, but she blocked my way. I needed time to think. Time to figure out what I was supposed to say. This wasn't the way the night was meant to end.

Where was Jude?

"You and Judith?" Mr Tremayne's voice was soft, yet it trembled with anger. "What do you mean, a hoax?"

"Judith wouldn't do that to us." Mrs Tremayne ('call me Ruth' she had told me only a moment ago) was shaking her head. "No, Judith wouldn't do that to us. That would be too cruel."

I wanted to lie. Tell them I was mixed up, didn't know what I was saying, but I had said too much already. And Mrs Tremayne's eyes were puffy with tears and I didn't want to lie any more and hurt her. Judith had told me they were heartless. I had seen none of that. All I had witnessed was two people whose hearts were breaking. And I couldn't take seeing it any more.

Jude didn't have to watch that heartbreak. I hadn't thought it would be like this. I hadn't realised it would hurt her parents so much. That it would hurt me so much. Why hadn't she told me?

All this went through my mind in the blink of an eye.

"This was all a trick?" Mrs Tremayne took a step back from me, as if I had suddenly become contagious.

I found my voice at last. "Not a trick... It wasn't meant to be a trick. She was going to come back tonight, in the middle of all this; you would be reunited with your daughter. Happy ending all round. You would never know. No one would know."

"But why did she do this? Why did you do this?"

That couldn't be told in a sentence. And why did we do it? I needed time to think.

Mrs Tremayne gripped my arm, her fingers digging in so hard it hurt. "Where is Judith? Where has she been all this time?"

"I don't know," and that was true. Jude had never told me where she was going to be. She'd said if I didn't know where she was hiding out, I couldn't give it away with a thoughtless word or gesture. But she'd said she had a place – a safe place.

It looked as if the crowd had all come back to the street, surging forward. News of my revelation had spread, whisper upon whisper, growing louder by the second. I could hear them.

"What's all this about?"

"Did she say it was a hoax?"

"We're at a blinkin' candlelit vigil for nothing."

"Treating us like muppets."

The camera was still on me. I tried to cover my face, to hide it, and Sara Flynn was still asking questions.

"Did you and Judith come up with this? Was that the plan? She would pretend to go missing, and you would pretend to do your best to bring her back? Why? Why would you do such a thing?"

As the crowd started to grasp the story of the evening, they began to boo. A moment ago they were cheering me, applauding me. And now they were booing. There was nothing but disgust in their eyes.

"I want to go home," I mumbled.

Mr Tremayne took my arm. "No way. I'm calling the police." I tried to pull apart from him, but his wife took my other arm.

"You're coming with us."

TWELVE

The police came. It seemed only moments later. I hadn't even heard Mr Tremayne calling them. Had someone in the crowd called them? They arrived in a car, which brought a few more neighbours out onto the street to join the crowd. Jude's mum was still crying in my ear, her dad was shouting, "Where is Judith!" and "How could you do this to us?" Over and over.

And Sara Flynn bombarding me. "How did you come up with this? Whose idea was it?"

It all merged into one big buzz of words.

This couldn't be happening. I felt sick. This wasn't the way it was meant to be.

I was led into the police car, with neighbours and pupils – they'd all kept hanging about – hissing and booing at me, shouting threats and insults, and even as the car pulled away they were shaking their fists at me, a couple even ran towards the car and starting ramming on the windows, on the bonnet. I was scared the glass would break and they would drag me outside. I was shaking.

Dad was waiting for me at the station, and in the middle of all this I still thought: he hadn't made it to the vigil like he said he would.

"No wonder you didn't want me there," were his first words. Almost his only words. He could hardly speak to me, hardly look at me, but I saw that his eyes welled up with tears. Tears of anger and of shame. "How could you do this, Abbie? Why?"

"It was Judith's idea," I told him, and I said it to the police again in the interview room. "Judith had read online about these two girls in America. One had pretended to go missing, and the other had 'found' all the clues to eventually trace her. When the missing girl came back, Judith said they were both celebrated. They became famous and it was only years later it all came out that it was a hoax. And Judith thought, we thought, how much better it would work now, with mobile phones and messaging and social media and everything, and she'd come back on the night of the candlelit vigil, and no one would ever know what we'd done."

"But why would you want to do such a cruel thing, Abbie?" Dad butted in even when the police officer held up a hand, signalling him to be quiet.

"Jude said her parents were awful, she hated them, and… and if she stayed away they would realise how much they missed her." She had told me that, and I had believed her. "And you spend so much time fighting for other people, I wanted you to notice me too. I wanted to do something that would make you see me. Make you proud of me."

He gasped as if I'd hit him in the face. He sat back. But it was true; he had to know it was true.

"Jude said her parents deserved it. They didn't care about her."

"And do you believe that now?"

I shook my head. "I don't know why she said such a thing."

"She did all this to hurt her parents?"

"No, not just that. She had these friends and they had dumped her. And she was really upset about that."

I didn't mention Andrea or Tracey or Belinda's names. The police would find out who they were. Jude had been shoved out, deserted, excluded, and I knew how that felt. Not that she had welcomed my sympathy.

"You haven't a clue how I feel," she had snapped at me. So I didn't tell her about how my mum had died, and my dad had drowned himself in union work and didn't seem to notice I was grieving too.

But that day was the beginning of little talks, secretive phone calls and coming up with this plan – while everyone still thought we hardly knew each other.

"Do you always do what a so-called friend tells you?" My dad wasn't going to stop the grilling.

"I don't think so," I murmured. I'd never thought of myself as someone who could be manipulated, but if I wasn't, then I had no explanation of why I had done this terrible thing.

"Still, you insist this was Jude's idea?"

"Ok, ok, mine too. I agreed with it." I so wanted to reach out and grab his hand but I was sure he would snatch it away.

The policewoman asked me the next question: "So her parents deserved it, your dad deserved it, her friends deserved it... What about William Creen?"

I had almost forgotten William Creen.

"Someone told me about him. I'd never heard of him. I don't know anything about him." And who was that someone? I just couldn't remember.

The WPC leaned across the table towards me. "And she was going to come home tonight, welcomed with open arms, and you, you would be the heroine of the hour."

Happy ending all round, Jude had said when we planned it. *What could go wrong?*

You didn't come back, Jude, that's what went wrong.

"And what was going to be her story when she came back?"

"She was going to say she ran away because of a fight with her parents." A fight she had deliberately picked, but I said nothing about that. "And she had stayed away because..."

"Because why?"

"She was going to say she thought someone was stalking her, someone was frightening her."

"So William Creen was the perfect stooge."

I was shaking my head. "No, she wasn't going to name anyone. She never mentioned William Creen. It was just an excuse for not coming back."

"Which just means Willam Creen would always have been under suspicion."

I couldn't stop the tears then. "I know, I know, it was a terrible thing to do, but at the time it seemed..."

What word could I use? Harmless? Fun? Nothing fitted. Nothing was good enough. No word was bad enough. I turned to my dad then. "I'm so sorry, Dad."

"So where is Judith now? And why didn't she come back?"

"I swear I don't know. She was meant to come back tonight, during the candlelit vigil."

Suddenly Dad was shouting at me, "Abbie! If you know where that girl is, just tell us."

He was angry. Though I knew he was a firebrand at marches and meetings, I so seldom saw him angry.

"I don't know, Dad. Honest. I swear on Mum's grave. I don't know."

I said sorry a thousand times that night. At the beginning of the night I had been so hopeful. It was going to be over. I had had enough of it by then. I just wanted it to be over. I had hated lying to Jude's mum and dad. I hadn't realised how hard it would be, lying to everyone, pretending. A laugh at first, but it soon turned into a nightmare. I hadn't realised, either, how much I would like people liking me. Or how guilty I would feel that I was fooling them, that it was all a lie.

And nothing had turned out the way we had planned. I'd be apologising for the rest of my life, because they were all right. We had done a terrible thing, Jude and I.

It should be over.

It was meant to be over.

But where was Jude?

THIRTEEN

4_Eva9900

Abbie Kerr is a lying cow

468 💬 357 💙 131 💬

Princess4581 commented:

OMG have you heard what she's done?! #LyingCow #AbbieKerr

32 💙

---

gr8estcc4 commented:

She's such a #liar. Trying to make us look like idiots.

96 💙

Glasgow_Grl commented:

I hate her #LyingCow

387 💙

I didn't want to go to school the next day. I begged Dad to let me stay off. He wouldn't let me. He was set like stone. "You'll just have to face the music," he said.

But why should *I* face the music and not Jude? It so wasn't fair. So I planned to skidge school. Set off in the morning, pretend to go, then just come back home, wrap myself in a duvet and try to forget. Dad must have read my mind. "Never mind getting the bus. I'll take you to school."

He didn't even stop on the road so I could sneak away before the school gates. He drove right into the plaza, as close as he could get to the front doors, and drew to a halt in a disabled bay.

"Aren't you going to work?" I asked him.

Dad never took time off work. Even when Mum died he hardly took any time off. I could never understand that.

"Oh yes, I'm going into work. I've got to face the music there too." He turned to look right at me. "Do you know, yesterday I was that proud of you. People were slapping me on the back, calling you a wee heroine… and now…"

I hated that I had made him so unhappy. When he looked at me I had never seen his eyes so cold.

"So you will go to school and you will apologise to everyone."

Some of the pupils waiting in the cold for the bell to ring had turned when Dad's car come to a halt. I'd seen their expressions change when they saw who was arriving.

I began to breathe faster. "I think I'm hyper-ventilating," I said, my breath coming in short bursts, "or I'm having a heart attack."

"You can't die of shame," Dad said. He didn't even look at me. He kept his eyes fixed on the steering wheel. I wanted to reach out and touch him, but I knew he'd only draw away. From somewhere, I found the courage to open the car door.

There should have been noise in the playground. Instead, the world was silent, as if the mute button had been pressed. All eyes were aimed at me, like daggers. I closed the car door and Dad screeched into reverse, desperate to get away from me. I watched the car until it disappeared down the long drive and out of the school gates. The maroon and yellow ties still hung there, not fluttering now, but drooped and looking pathetic in the rain. I forced myself to start walking, sure my legs wouldn't hold up. That was when the volume turned up to full blast. I was yelled at, shouted at, called the most horrible names. I began to run, and it only got worse. They pelted me with cartons, plastic bottles, half-eaten sandwiches, anything they could get their hands on. I ran towards the school entrance, but inside there were more pupils waiting for me. All equally vicious.

"I cannot believe even you could do that," Belinda sneered.

"You're worse than a monster." Tracey almost spat the words out.

I tried to dodge past her but Andrea stepped in front of me. "How could you come up with something like that? You're pure evil."

I wanted to shout back some smart, clever

comeback, but I couldn't, because she was right. What we'd done was evil.

"I was really beginning to think you were ok. I was telling everybody we'd got you all wrong." Andrea turned to her friends, "Wasn't I?" And they all nodded. "I cannot believe what you've done."

It was Mr Barr who saved me. If you could call it being saved. He came to the bottom of the stairs, his molten-candle face grim. "Abbie Kerr, my office. Now."

"Now you're for it," Andrea whispered.

"You'll get the jail for this," Tracey giggled. "At least I hope so."

Big Belinda snapped after me, "They should throw away the key."

"This is a very serious business, Abbie." Mr Barr sat at his desk. Left me standing in front of it. My throat hurt holding back the tears. But crying wouldn't gain me any sympathy, and everyone would think that was the reason for my tears: begging for sympathy that I wouldn't get. So I stood with my rucksack on my hip, staring ahead. Did I look arrogant? Not the least bit sorry? Bet I did. Habit of a lifetime.

"You made a fool of everyone, Abbie. A candlelit vigil, school ties on the gates. You used the good intentions of all your friends."

What friends? I wanted to ask. The only time I'd had 'friends' was while this was going on. While they thought I was doing something wonderful. I had liked that feeling. Now, once again, I had no friends. I had enemies.

"And where's Judith now? You must know."

I was so fed up with being asked that question. "Honest sir, I don't know where she's been all week. She wouldn't tell me. She was meant to come back last night, sir. At the vigil... I don't know why she didn't come. That's all I can tell you."

"You realise, Abbie, no one is ever going to believe you again." I kept my eyes down, didn't want to face him. "And yet, I am going to order you to do one last thing."

My heart chilled. What was he going to order me to do?

"You've abused the facilities of this school for your own ends, and you will certainly never be allowed to use them again." He paused. "After today. Today you will go from this office to the studio, where you will be filmed apologising to the whole school."

My legs shook. I wanted to sit down. This was utter humiliation. "I can't."

"You can, and you will. I've been on the phone to your father and asked his permission, and he agrees it is something you should do."

My dad had agreed to this?

He went on, "If you could step in front of a camera and ask the whole school to pray for Judith, to look for Judith, to come to a vigil, then it should be just as easy for you to do the same thing to apologise."

I shook my head. I still couldn't believe he was going to make me do this.

He stood up. "I was planning to suspend you, Abbie, but you know, I think a worse punishment for you would be coming to school and facing everyone, everyone you have let down, day after day."

I followed him from his office in silence. My legs were like rubber. Bubbles of air floated in front of my eyes. I was sure I was going to faint. I wanted to leap over the banister and race for the front doors. Yet still I followed him. The corridors were empty. Everyone was in class. I prayed no one would be at the studio. That I could maybe pretend no one was going to see me, or hear me.

But that day none of my prayers were answered. Angus was waiting as if he'd known I was coming. Like the hangman knows when a condemned prisoner is led from a cell. He stood up when I came in. He looked nervous.

Even worse, Robbie was there too.

"Have we got to be in the same room as her!" It wasn't a question. It was a demand. "Phoney bitch."

"Watch your language, Robbie," Mr Barr warned him.

"How could you do it, Abbie?" Angus looked disgusted, as if even saying my name put a bad taste in his mouth.

"She wanted to be a star, eh, Abbie? Wee bit of publicity. On television, front page of the paper, eh?" Robbie didn't know when to shut up.

The head didn't even stop him this time. All he said was, "She is to be on air for only a few minutes. All she is allowed to do is apologise. Nothing else."

"And of course, everybody's gonny believe her apology." Robbie came closer. "Nobody is ever gonny believe a word you say ever again."

How different this was to the last time I appeared on the school news feed. I had felt so clever, smug, even knowing I was lying through my teeth and that

I was taking everyone in. I didn't feel smug this time. Now I was so ashamed, contrite. But mixed in with that, I was angry. Judith was as much to blame as I was. Where was she?

Where did it come from, what I said that day? No script. No real warning, yet every word came from the bottom of my heart.

"I want to tell you all how sorry I am about lying to you. I don't know why Jude and me thought it would be such a great idea. I didn't realise it would hurt so many people. I knew she was safe, but nobody else did and I should have seen it would hurt her mum and dad especially, and now I don't know where Jude is and I'm the one who's scared. I deserve you all to hate me. I'm sorry. I'm so sorry."

It was all I said – all I was allowed to say. Mr Barr drew his finger across his throat to shut me up. The camera clicked off. Only then was I allowed to go, and as soon as I walked into the corridor: instant replay. There was my face, bigger than life, my voice coming from every screen in the school. I couldn't get away from it.

It was played over and over in a loop every break that day, but my apology made no difference to everyone's comments online.

grrlgrrl888

Did you see Abbie Kerr on the studio feed again? Can't believe a word she says, it's all for show. #LyingCow #AbbieKerr

276 🎬 312 ❤ 126 💬

---

andreaglass15 commented:

She loves being on screen, that's what it's all about. She's not sorry. #LyingCow #AbbieKerr

217 ❤

FOURTEEN

My nightmare never seemed to end. I had to pass people staring at me, calling me names, pushing against me so I stumbled. I had no one to turn to.

What was the point of apologising? I could almost hear Jude's voice in my ear: *I would have refused to apologise. They can't make you, you know. You've got rights.*

Of course I could have just told Mr Barr no. Why didn't I? Because my dad wanted me to do it, and because I was swamped with guilt at what we'd done, Jude and me. It was meant to be a stupid prank, a game that would make us both famous. How could we not have realised how cruel it would be?

I tried to console myself that it had been Jude's plan, right from the beginning. It *was* Jude who came up with the details. She would pick a fight with her parents, she said. Wouldn't be difficult, she was always arguing with them. Andrea and the others bullying her, dumping her – that would work as another reason for her disappearance. Girls were always running away for less, she said. "No one even knows we're friends, so they won't suspect anything." I'd always thought Jude was a bit stupid, but she was clever coming up with all this.

I had known nothing about this Creen man, hadn't even heard of him. That wasn't my fault. Someone had said Jude thought he was always watching her, and I just passed that on.

But then, Jude always thought she was being watched, being admired, being envied. Swishing her long hair over her shoulder, pouting her lips. How had I ever thought we could be friends? We had nothing in common.

It was me all on my own who had come up with the candlelit vigil and the dramatic moment for her return. All me. And that all failed.

I had been worse than a fool to agree to do what I had done, I had been selfish and cruel and I had let someone manipulate me. But I had been unhappy. As unhappy as Jude. That was my excuse. I had no friends at this school, no one liked me, and Dad... Dad was never there for me.

Had this been Jude's plan all along: not to appear when she was meant to? So I would be left to face everyone's anger, alone? I almost hoped that was true, because if it wasn't… did that mean something awful had happened to her? Where was she?

The police weren't finished with me yet. They came to the house the next day after school. Dad was there, home early for once, but he might as well have been miles away for all he talked to me.

The two officers told me there was a very good chance I would be charged with wasting police time. "It will go to the Procurator Fiscal for his decision. It really all depends on where Judith is, and why she hasn't come home."

"Where has she been all this time?"

They were trying to catch me in a lie. I had already told them I didn't know. "She said she had somewhere safe to go, to stay. That was all she told me."

"So Judith was in charge of the whole plan? It was all her idea?"

I so wanted to yell: YES! But I had gone along with her plan. I'd put it into action. Deep down I knew I deserved as much blame as she did.

"Did neither of you stop to think what this would do to her parents?"

I remembered Jude, in a corner of a cafe in Kilmacolm. We had taken separate buses to get there, far away from where anyone knew us. "My mum and dad deserve it, Abbie," she had said. "They've hurt me so much, and I don't think they really care about me any more."

She'd even cried.

Now that I had met her parents, I knew they were nothing like how Jude had painted them.

I had to hold back my tears, because if Jude's crying back there in Kilmacolm seemed false to me now, how phoney would my tears look to the police?

I felt sick by the time they left. Dad and I ate our dinner in silence. He couldn't talk to me. There was nothing to say; I had told him everything I could and no amount of sorry would ever be enough to make things better.

If Jude would just come back, we could at least share the blame. I tossed and turned all that night. What if she couldn't come back? A chill ran through me every time I thought of that. What if something really awful had happened to her? Would I ever sleep again?

Next day at school I was a laughing stock. As soon as I walked in through the entrance I could see why.

The photo I had been so proud of, the one of me on the front page of the local paper, was up on the big screen, and somebody had messed my face right up. It showed me with blackened teeth and a Hitler moustache. My eyes had been darkened so I looked sinister and evil. The photo was taken down, reluctantly I'm sure, before lunchtime. And I was just as sure that Robbie was behind it. Always clever with I.T.

But that photo coming down didn't make things any better for me. One of the fourth-year boys stormed up to me as I waited in the cafe queue at lunch. He had a group of friends with him who looked as angry as he did.

He pulled me round to face him. "Where is she? Where's that blinkin' Jude Tremayne? Tell her to get back here!"

I shook my head. "I'm so sorry. I don't know. I wish I did. I would tell you if I did."

"My wee uncle's under suspicion. The police have had him in for questioning." It was Josh Creen, William Creen's nephew. I vaguely remembered the name. "And he will be under suspicion until she comes back. So you get her here!" He lifted his fist.

"If I could beat the information out of you, I would." He looked around. "And nobody would stop me."

One of his friends pulled him away. "She's not worth it."

But he was still shouting: "You're going to get what's coming to you for this, Abbie Kerr! You hear me? You're going to be sorry."

Everyone sitting in the cafe looked more amused than outraged. Josh was right. He could have beaten me to a pulp and no one would have stopped him. I got my lunch and carried my tray up to an empty table. I had no choice anyway. No one moved to let me sit with them.

I looked around the cafe as I played with my macaroni cheese. Only a few days ago they were all surrounding me with their friendship, relying on me for answers. I had felt like a leader. And now?

They hated me.

Tracey was walking up towards me, and she was actually smiling. Was someone going to understand what I was going through?

She stopped at my table. "Are you ok, Abbie?"

I was so grateful for her concern I could only smile back. She leaned down to me, touched my hand. "I just wanted to say... enjoy your lunch."

And she spat on my plate.

FIFTEEN

Over the next couple of days I grew to understand why teenagers can have thoughts of suicide. They were the worst days of my life. At least when my mum died I had people to comfort me. My Auntie Ellen was always there for me. She's my mum's sister and another of the reasons we moved to Port Glasgow. She lives in Gourock, just down the river. I so wished she was here now, but she was off on some long adventure holiday in the Australian outback. I couldn't even call her. Would I want to? No, in a way I was glad she wasn't here. I'd be too ashamed to talk to her.

I had no one. No friends, my dad ignoring me. It seemed only the media were interested in me. There were constant phone calls and messages asking for interviews. When calls came at home, Dad wouldn't even speak, he'd just slam the phone down angrily, then glare at me. I dreaded seeing the papers. Sara Flynn was still trying to get in touch. I had heard she was almost camping outside Jude's house now, waiting for her return. I was sure I would be charged with wasting police time. But if Jude came back, at least she would be charged too.

I was getting texts from Mrs Tremayne:

Jude's Mum

> If you know where she is, please tell me. I'll make sure you don't get into trouble for it. Ruth Tremayne

> Please, if you know, tell the police.

It would all have died down, except Jude was still missing. And that's what stopped me having serious thoughts about harming myself. I had to know why she hadn't come back.

I saw Mr and Mrs Tremayne on television at yet another press conference, begging for their daughter's return. I cried as I watched them.

"Judith, if you can hear me, please come back. We love you, we won't blame you for anything. Just come home."

Was she listening, watching them? William Creen was on the news bulletin too, shown coming out of the police station, chalk white, eyes down. "Helping police with their enquiries."

"Did you see Jude's mum on telly last night?" Andrea grabbed me as soon as I walked in through the school entrance. Tracey and Belinda closed ranks around her. "Does that make you feel proud?"

I managed to get away from them, but as I walked up the stairs to my first class it occurred to me that Jude was seen as a victim. She wasn't being blamed for anything. She'd been my partner in crime, but nobody was blaming her. Just me.

I was in class when my phone buzzed in my pocket. Someone was sending me a text. Probably Sara Flynn, asking again for an interview. I didn't take the phone out till class was over and I was in the corridor. And then I checked who it was from. It just said 'UNKNOWN'.

UNKNOWN

Help me Abbie It's Jude

SIXTEEN

The phone shook in my trembling hand. My head swam.

UNKNOWN

> Help me Abbie It's Jude

Of course I tried to call back, send another message, but it was no good. No caller ID. Unknown.

Why wasn't she using her own phone? Whose phone was the message coming from? Was it really Jude?

I didn't even realise I was running, pushing past annoyed pupils, taking the stairs two at a time, rushing for the head's office. I was vaguely aware of the strange looks I was getting as I ran. I was breathing heavily, my stomach was doing somersaults. I must have looked like I was crazy. I didn't knock. I barged right past his secretary and pushed my way into Mr Barr's office.

"What do you think you're doing, Abbie?" The secretary jumped up, but I was already in. Mr Barr sat at his desk, papers spread out around him. He looked up and I held the phone right in his face.

"Look! Look what I just got! It's from Jude."

He took the phone in his thick stubby fingers, held it at a distance as if he might catch something from it. He read the message. Must have read it twice considering how long it took him to turn his eyes and look back at me.

"Is this another of your practical jokes?"

"No sir. It's Jude, she says she needs help."

"Really." His voice was calm and cold. "You think we're going to fall for that one again?"

How could I make him believe me? "It is Jude." Did I sound convincing? "It must be. It has to be her."

"Conveniently coming from an unknown number."

"Maybe..." I was trying to think of an explanation. "Maybe she lost her own phone, maybe this is the only one she could get." Even to me it sounded weak.

"So she loses her own phone, but manages to find another, or perhaps she bought it somewhere? Or, more likely, you've had someone send you a message from an unknown number."

He handed me back the phone.

"Do you think anyone would do that for me?" Did he forget I was the hated Abbie Kerr? I tried to keep calm, but I couldn't let it go. "What if it is Jude? She needs help. We've got to do something."

"Too bad she didn't leave a number then." He stood up. "I'll let this go this time, Abbie. But this better be the last."

The secretary was ushering me out.

"Jude's still missing; we can't take any chances."

But it was no good. "Ever heard of the boy who cried wolf, Abbie?"

I stumbled to my next class. I wanted to blurt out to everyone about the text, but I knew their reaction would be the same as the head's. They'd say it was another hoax.

After school, I missed the bus, and I ran all the way home down the long winding road to the shore while October darkness gathered about me. Someone had to believe me. I prayed my dad would be home from work. I'd show him the text. He would do something.

I was so relieved to see his car in the drive. I burst into the house. He was in the living room reading the paper. "Dad, Dad, look what I got."

I showed him the message, and stood trembling while he read it. His face betrayed nothing. It could have been made of stone.

"Is this the second part of your cunning plan?" he asked.

"What plan?"

"Well, first she goes missing, and you say she's coming back, and she doesn't, so then she really is missing. Then: Abracadabra! Another message. Help me! And you can be the hero who finds her again?"

"This is for real, Dad. Honest."

I'd never seen my dad look at me with such disgust before. "I wish I could believe you, Abbie. But if I don't, no one else will. And at the moment I'm having a hard time believing anything you say."

I wouldn't let it go. "Whether you believe me or not, Jude is still missing. Someone has to take this seriously. I want you to call the police. If you don't, I'll do it myself."

He handed me the phone. "You better call them then."

The same two police constables who had questioned me before came to the house: a man and a woman. I hardly let them get in before I was rattling off the whole story, pushing the phone at them, desperate to make them believe me. "It has to be Jude. It has to be."

"Why wouldn't she use her own phone?"

Same question all the time. Same answer. "I don't know. Maybe she lost it." It was their job to follow this up. I bit my lip as I watched them read and reread the text.

"What's all this?"

The WPC held the phone out to me.

"What?" But I hardly needed to look. I realised what she'd been reading.

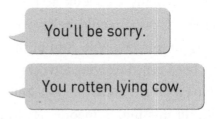

You'll be sorry.

You rotten lying cow.

She had scrolled through some of the hate messages I had received over the past few days. "They're all sending them to me. Half the school. More. All the time. I don't blame them, but... should

102

I have reported it?" Here I was, still thinking they might have a little concern for me.

"Seems to me one, or maybe more than one, of your so-called friends is pulling your leg. They shouldn't be, but we can all understand why it's happening."

"Aren't you even going to investigate? Can't you take the phone, find out where the text came from?"

"This isn't the CSI, Abbie. We're the Greenock polis."

"You would have before," I reminded them.

"We believed you before. But we don't stretch to that, not for a hoax."

My dad snatched the phone from the policewoman. "Thank you, officers," he said. "We'll delete the text, and the other messages here. Any more of this nonsense, Abbie, and I'll take the phone away from you altogether."

SEVENTEEN

It was all around the school next day that I had received a text from an unknown number supposedly coming from Jude. How had they found out? Who had told them?

I didn't know. All I knew was it made things a lot harder for me.

This time it was Belinda who pulled me aside in the corridor. "Not had enough attention? Just want to hurt her family some more. Kiddin' on you've heard from her."

She wasn't the only one who ranted at me. Most of the others gathering around her had something to say.

Finally, I let rip. "Jude's missing. Really missing now. She really does need help this time. We've got to do something!"

Belinda had the ugliest laugh I'd ever heard, a big deep-throated laugh that made her sound like a man. "Oh, what do you suggest, Abbie? Ties round the railings? A candlelit vigil? I'd rather tie *you* round the railings."

And everyone laughed at her little joke.

Of course they wouldn't believe me. I was the only one who knew the truth: Jude was supposed to come back and she didn't. She might really be in trouble now. But how could I help her if no one would listen to me?

I decided to ask Angus. He was older, a really nice guy. He hadn't been as cruel as the rest when the story of the hoax came out. He was the one person I could think of who might understand and give me some advice at least. I found him at break time in the library. He was sitting with some of the other fifth years. When I approached their table, they either glared at me or just turned their backs, but Angus didn't.

"Can I talk to you for a minute, Angus?" I motioned for him to move away from the table – I didn't want the others to hear.

He stood up and stepped towards me. "Is this about the text you got?"

I nodded. "It came from an unknown number, but it said it was from Jude. I don't know what to do."

"Have you shown it to the police?"

"Of course."

"And did they believe you?"

I didn't have to answer that directly. "I suppose I can't blame them."

"No, you can't," he agreed.

"But what if she's really in trouble? How do I help her? What do I do?"

He didn't say anything for a moment. I hoped he was thinking over my options. Some hope.

"You've burned your boats, Abbie. Jude too. Nobody's going to take the chance that this might be another trick and you're going to make a fool of everybody again."

"But this time…" I didn't get it finished.

Angus shrugged his shoulders and turned back to his friends.

He was right. No matter what text Jude sent, no one was going to believe it was real. If I wanted to help Jude, I could only rely on myself. But how?

Where are you, Jude? I sent up a silent prayer. Please be safe, Jude.

As I left the library, there was Robbie. Had he

been waiting for me? How much had he heard? From what he said first, it was clear he had heard enough. "Thought Angus would be a soft touch, eh? Think again. Angus isn't as daft as he looks."

"Not as daft looking as you anyway." I tried to move past him but he blocked my way.

"Abbie, see the number of people in this school who hate you? Who wouldn't spit on you if you were on fire? I'd stop counting after a hundred. Any of them could have sent you the text. Let me see it?" He held out his hand for my phone. I hesitated, and his face broke into a slow smile. "Ah, if there even was a text. Make that up as well, did you?"

I shouted at him. "I showed it to the head, to my dad, the police."

He beckoned me with his fingers. "Come on then. Show us."

I couldn't look him in the eye. "My dad made me delete all my texts and messages. Right!"

There was something dark in his smile now. Something vicious. A Robbie smile I had not seen before. "How handy. The disappearing text. Know what you need, Abbie?" His face came close to mine. "A taste of your own medicine. See how you like it."

He knocked against me as he walked past.

"Make sure you let us know the next time you don't get a text."

I was beginning to think I had imagined it myself. Had there ever been a text at all?

Dad *had* made me delete all my messages, but more kept flooding in.

> I see what you're up to now.

> We're on to you, Abbie.

> How do you like it?

> You won't make a fool of us again.

It got me thinking that maybe the police were right. Maybe the text was from another pupil, more than one. Possibly all of them.

Who hated me? Ha! What had Robbie said? Stop counting after a hundred.

But that night I tossed and turned. Because even if the text was a hoax on me, Jude was still missing.

Why had she changed our plan? If she'd come back when she was meant to, it would have worked perfectly. She, the prodigal daughter would have been welcomed with open arms, and I'd have been the heroine of the day, and together we'd be famous, just like she'd wanted. It had all seemed so simple. (How could I not have seen it would be cruel?) Something must have stopped her, something kept her from coming back that night.

Still, she could send a message to anyone, to everyone, ten different kinds of messages, and if she was genuinely in trouble she could call her own parents. So why would she contact me?

Sometime in the middle of the night, the ping on the phone woke me. I snatched it up from my bedside table. The text seemed to stand out in metre-high illuminated letters.

UNKNOWN

HELP ME ABBIE JUDE

EIGHTEEN

I almost flew out of bed ready to run into Dad's room. Stopped dead before I reached the door. I remembered Dad's words. He had warned me that he would take my phone away if I mentioned anything like this again. I could see him deleting this text too. Then no one would believe there had ever been one.

I sat on the edge of the bed while darkness gave way to the dull grey light of a Scottish morning, and I tried to work out what I should do. There were only two people who were so desperate for news that they would jump at anything, every chance of gaining any scrap of information about their daughter: Jude's mum and dad. I made my decision. I would take the phone to them. They would know someone who could perhaps trace the text. People were so anxious to help them, they could easily find an expert.

And then they would find Jude, and maybe, just maybe, this terrible burden of guilt would be lifted from me. Or would at least be shared.

Usually, Dad went off to work, and I left a little after him to catch my bus. But that day I didn't head for the bus stop. Instead, I made my way to Jude's house. I knew I was the last person her mum and dad wanted to see, but I had to make them listen, and when they did, when they saw the text, they would be grateful. Taking the shortcut through the back lanes and the waste ground, it only took ten minutes. I slouched through the rain with my hood pulled up over my head. I didn't want any of the neighbours recognising me.

The last time I had been on Jude's street, flames had glowed in the darkness, sparks had risen to the midnight-blue sky. Mrs Tremayne had hugged me and called me a heroine and told me to call her Ruth. I had seen nothing but warmth and admiration in everyone's eyes.

It could have been such a wonderful memory, but I knew, too, how guilty I had felt. Because it was all a lie, I was fooling everyone and I hated myself for it. I had prayed for the moment when Jude would appear through the crowd and it would all be over.

Today an ice-cold wind ruffled the river. The sky was battleship grey. I hoped one of her parents would be in, that they hadn't both gone off to work. My hands shook as I reached for the doorbell. I heard it ring out through the house, and with trembling fingers I clicked on the text on my phone, opened it, ready to show them. I needed to make sure it was still there. I planned to hold it out before they could slam the door in my face.

UNKNOWN

HELP ME ABBIE
JUDE

It was Mr Tremayne who opened the door. He saw me, and drew back. "Not you. You've been warned to stay away from us."

I shoved the phone in his face. "Jude's been texting me. Look!"

"I don't want any more of your lies."

"They're not lies, not this time. Look. This is the second text I've had. It has to be Jude."

Mrs Tremayne came rushing down the stairs to the door. "I know that voice. Get the hell away from here."

But her husband had had time to think. He had taken the phone from me. He was studying the text. I could see his mind ticking over. Could this be Judith? Or was it another trick?

He didn't flinch as Mrs Tremayne hauled him aside to get at me. "How dare you come back here?"

I was sure she was about to slap me. I stepped back. "I've had a text from Jude."

"Another lie! Another lie!" she screamed at me. There was a sob in her voice and dark circles under her eyes. She looked as if she hadn't slept in days. No make-up, her skin grey, her hair unkempt.

What had we done to this poor woman, me and Jude?

"I'm not lying, and I can't know if it is definitely Jude, but it says it is, and I had to come and show you… just in case."

"It says UNKNOWN." Mr Tremayne's voice was flat. He handed the phone to his wife. "We should take it to the police."

I was reluctant to tell them, but had no choice. "They won't help. I showed them the last one and they didn't believe it was real."

"There's been more than one? And you didn't come and tell us?"

"Just the one, and I took it to the police."

"Is this a trick, Abbie? Because we can't take any more."

"No, no." I wanted to cry. I didn't blame them thinking what they were thinking. Still, I knew they would cling to any hope.

"Come in." Mr Tremayne stood aside to let me pass, and when his wife objected he stopped her with a gentle touch on her lips. "We can't take any chances."

For the first time, I felt I had done the right thing. I walked into their living room. I didn't sit down. I wasn't offered a seat anyway. I stood with my back against the wall while Mr Tremayne called the police. He took the phone into the kitchen so all I heard was a mumble of words. A few minutes later he came out. "They're going to take the phone and see if they can find out anything from it." He looked at me coldly. "They're doing this very reluctantly. They don't believe it's real. They think it's some pupils hoaxing you. Just as you hoaxed them."

"I know."

"They're doing this for us. Last resort. But if you're lying, Abbie..."

"No. Honest. I don't know if it is Jude, but if it is she might really need help."

Mrs Tremayne let out a little gasp and sank bonelessly down on the chair. "Oh my God."

Almost at that same moment the doorbell rang again.

The police here so soon?

Mr Tremayne hurried to answer it. I saw him take a step back when he took in who it was.

Sara Flynn, with her trusty cameramen beside her, already filming. Of course – hadn't I heard they were practically parked on the Tremayne's doorstep?

"What are you doing here?" Mr Tremayne asked.

Sara Flynn didn't answer. She peered into the house and saw me. She didn't look surprised. She'd obviously spotted me coming in. "Is this about the text? It was all over social media yesterday."

She was talking about that first text. She couldn't know about the second.

Mrs Tremayne grabbed my arm so tightly it hurt. "Is this why you're doing this? You want back on television. Is this what this is all about?"

"No!" I pulled myself free of her and made for the door. "Go away. Please," I told Sara. I stepped outside, kept trying to push her away.

Sara looked beyond me to Jude's mum.

"Do you believe the text is from your daughter, Mrs Tremayne?"

It was Mr Tremayne who answered. You could see he was holding in his anger. "I'd really like you to go."

I was on the path now, outside the house, and Sara Flynn had stepped outside with me. But there was some kind of commotion at the end of the street – shouts and yells – and both of us turned to look.

Neighbours were already at their doors, they'd seen the tv people arriving and going into the house. It was those neighbours who saw her first. They were the ones who were shouting.

Then we all looked. Mrs Tremayne pulled me aside so she could see.

There, stumbling down the street, looking bedraggled and upset, was Jude.

NINETEEN

I was in a silent movie. I could hear nothing – not the traffic passing, not Mrs Tremayne's scream as she ran past me. I saw papers cartwheeling down the street in the wind, a couple of seagulls fighting over some chips dropped on the pavement. Sara Flynn running after Mrs Tremayne, the cameraman behind her at the ready.

And I saw Jude.

She seemed to be walking in slow motion. Her hair was wild, flying all around her, her face looked dirty. She didn't so much walk as stagger, and by the time her mother caught up with her, Jude seemed to collapse into her arms. Then her dad was there, cradling both of them, leading them home.

And Sara Flynn captured it all for the lunchtime news. Some of the neighbours had their phones out filming too.

The family seemed unaware of anyone else. Jude was nestled in her mother's arms. Neighbours began to applaud.

I stepped back into the house. I thought I'd be shaking but I was so calm. The tears were streaming down my face, but I was calm. She was back. She was safe. It really was over now – that was all I could think. No one noticed me as they came inside. I tried to melt into the wall, hoping they wouldn't see me and ask me to leave. Surely I had every right to be here? To find out why she hadn't come back when she was supposed to, and where she'd been all the time she'd been away.

Sara Flynn followed them in, cameraman behind her with his camera still running. It took a moment for Jude's dad to realise she was there. He held up his hands. "Please, just go."

It was his wife who stopped him. "No. Let them stay. I want everyone to know she's back, and how relieved we are and," her voice broke into a sob, "how happy she's safe, and to thank everyone for their prayers and good wishes." Saying it seemed to exhaust her. She sank back on the sofa beside Jude. "But why Jude, why? How could you hurt us like this?"

Her father stepped in again. "Please stop filming, this is priva—" he didn't get to finish.

"I didn't want to, Mum. I didn't. I'm so sorry."

I should have shut up then, not said a word. They had forgotten me. I should have made sure it stayed that way. But no, I had to open my mouth. "I've told them Jude, they know everything. I've told them how sorry we are." I stepped forward. "But why didn't you come back when you were supposed to?"

It was as if she hadn't seen me before. She looked at me, her eyes went wide; her mouth fell open. "What? What is she doing here?" she gripped her mother's hand. "What are you talking about, Abbie Kerr?"

"I came about the text you sent, Jude. I wanted your mum and dad to see it; I wanted to help you."

"Text? What text?"

Her dad still had my phone. I nodded towards him. "The text you sent me. *HELP ME ABBIE*?"

"I didn't send you any text."

Her mother pulled her closer. "It doesn't matter, Jude. You're home."

No. It didn't matter. Jude was home. I didn't care about the text any more. "It must have been somebody winding me up then… But why didn't you come back, Jude?"

"You're asking me that?" she clung to her mother's arm, looked up into her eyes. "It was her that made me do it, Mum. It was all her idea." She got to her feet, unsteadily, though her mother tried to hold her down. "The only text I sent her was to say I wanted to come home… and *she* told me not to come back, she warned me." She moved towards me with such anger on her tear-stained face. "What have you been saying, Abbie?"

"I didn't warn you not to come back. That's a lie. Why are you saying that? Who were you afraid of, Jude?"

Her voice became almost hysterical. "Afraid of? Afraid of?" She pointed her finger right at me. "The only person I've ever been afraid of… is YOU!"

TWENTY

Now I was the one who was angry. This was all too much. "Afraid of me? You're talking bollocks. That's a lie. You know that."

"It was all her idea, Mum. She knew I was so unhappy about the girls falling out with me. She said we could make them sorry. She said it would make us famous. That's what she said." Jude was crying, but they were crocodile tears, I knew that now. "I should have said no, but I was scared to go against her. Then when I saw you and Dad on television and saw how it hurt you, Mum, I begged to come home. You must have known that when you saw the text: *I want to come home*. That's why I sent it. But she wouldn't let me."

I couldn't take in what I was hearing. Where was all this coming from?

Her mum was sitting her down again. "I know you were angry at us, I'm so sorry, we shouldn't have argued with you." I couldn't believe Mrs Tremayne was apologising. While Jude was lying through her teeth! I felt as if I'd fallen into some kind of alternative universe where nothing made sense.

"You didn't deserve this, Mum." Jude wiped her face with the palm of her hand.

She was landing me in so much trouble and no one was challenging her story.

"If you were so desperate to be home, why didn't you come back the night of the vigil – like we planned?"

There was a dramatic pause before she answered me. "Because it was so phoney, coming back like that." She burrowed her face into her mum's shoulder. "'Like the end of some Hollywood movie,' she said. 'It'll be great for publicity. It would look great on television' – that's what she said. My return would be captured on camera. But when it came to the night, I couldn't do it, Mum. I couldn't make a fool of so many people, they were all doing so much for me. Especially you. I wanted to come back quietly, just me."

Mrs Tremayne hugged her and looked at me with such cold fury I was silenced.

"I was going to call you... and then... she was telling everybody it was my idea, it was a hoax, and I was scared again. Scared to come back in case I'd get all the blame." She began sobbing again, comforted by her mother.

"If I was so scary, why were you sending me these?" I shoved my phone at her. "*HELP ME.* Why not send it to somebody else? Why not to your mum?"

She looked genuinely puzzled. I'd never realised what a good actress Jude was, but boy, she deserved an Oscar for this. "I didn't send that." She spoke to her dad now. "I didn't send that."

"And where have you been all this time?" I asked her.

She stared at me as if I had spoken in a foreign language. "What?"

"Where have you been?"

That was when she dropped another bombshell. "You know where I've been. It was you that told me where to go."

"Me?"

"Yes, you. I've been at your auntie's house in Gourock."

My breath caught in my throat. "What?"

Mrs Tremayne lost it then. "You've known all the time where she was, and you didn't tell us!"

I was shaking my head, still trying to take this in. "She wasn't at my auntie's house. That's another lie."

"No, no, it isn't," Jude said. "She was going to be away to Australia till February, you said. A safe place. You even gave me a key." While she was talking she was rummaging in the pocket of her jacket. Now she held it out. A key that looked identical to the one I kept in my rucksack. Auntie Ellen's key. "You gave it to me. You had a copy made." She turned to her mother. "She said there was plenty of food in her auntie's freezer."

She didn't have to convince her mother. If she'd said there were two moons in the sky, Mrs Tremayne would have believed every word.

"I'd never have let you stay in my auntie's house. Never."

"Well you did. And I can prove it. You phoned me on her landline. You said it was the safest way to get in touch with me."

Lie upon lie. I felt like jumping on her, bashing her. I made a move forward but her dad held me back. "I never phoned you."

"You did. The police'll be able to find your calls."

"I think you should get out of this house, now." There was such disgust in Mrs Tremayne's voice.

Mr Tremayne still held my arm. "No, I think she should stay. The police are on their way. I think Abbie's got a few questions to answer."

Jude began to shake. "No, Mum, no, I don't want to talk to the police. Not yet."

Her mum was the soft mark. "She's home safe. I'm going to run her a bath and then get her into bed. The police can come back later to talk to her."

"Well, I'm not staying," I said it as soon as Jude and her mother made a move to go upstairs, "and you can't make me."

Suddenly Sara Flynn was in my face. "Have you got anything to say about this, Abbie?" They'd been filming all the time. Invisible and unnoticed.

I shoved her away from me. "It's all lies. She's made it up." I ran past her and out into the street. Some of the neighbours were still there, and began hissing at me, as if they'd heard every word Jude said, as if they believed every word she'd said. After all, I had already been made out to be the villain, hadn't I?

I couldn't go to school. I was shaking. I couldn't figure out what was going on. I ran back the way I'd come, over the waste ground, my hood up.

All I'd wanted, all I'd thought I wanted, was Jude

home, safe and well. I knew a lot of that was so that she could share the burden of guilt I'd been carrying on my own. Now here she was back, and it was even worse.

Why was she saying these things? She was talking like she was the victim, and I was the big bad wolf.

TWENTY-ONE

Jude made the one o'clock news. Her return had been caught with perfect timing by Sara Flynn and her crew.

I watched it again, Jude stumbling down the windy street, while behind her the neighbours stepped out of doorways to see, and then Mrs Tremayne was running towards her. I could hear her sobs. She folded her daughter in her arms, and the neighbours erupted in applause. Over it, Sara Flynn's commentary: "This is an amazing moment. Judith Tremayne is home."

If only it had stopped there. But of course the biggest news was to come, and I was the main character.

There was footage of Jude crying and saying sorry to her mum. Her words sounded sincere and heartfelt.

Then there was a still picture of me looking dark and angry, my eyes wide, taken aback. Sara Flynn was saying: "There has been yet another shocking revelation in this unfolding story: Judith Tremayne has accused St Thomas's pupil, Abbie Kerr, of frightening her and making her stay away from home. A week ago, Abbie Kerr was celebrated for organising a campaign to find Judith, then on our news broadcast she confessed her involvement in the planned disappearance. Judith now says that Abbie Kerr has been aware of her whereabouts throughout the past weeks – knowledge Miss Kerr has persistently denied..."

Jude's face was tear-stained; the shot of me had such a sinister expression. Who would you have believed?

Jude's return was all over social media too, of course, with bumpy footage from the neighbours' phones. And Sara Flynn's 'revelation' was hardly out of her mouth on the tv when the messages began.

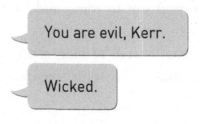

You are evil, Kerr.

Wicked.

Somebody's gonny get u 4 this.

You knew where she was all the time!

U r gonny b sorry.

I tried not to look at them but it was hard.

Dad came home as soon as he heard the news on the radio. "Is this true, Abbie. Was this all your idea?"

"No, it wasn't," I snapped at him. It hurt he could even think such a thing. "You think I could make Jude Tremayne do anything? That's a joke." I dreaded to tell him where Jude had been hiding. How had she got hold of my aunt's key? Even I couldn't understand it.

Still, I had to say something before the police came. And it shocked him as much as anything else.

"Did you give her a key?"

"Of course I didn't. It must be a lie," I said while he was still trying to take it in. "She couldn't have been there. I would never have given her Auntie Ellen's key."

"Why would she lie about a thing like that?"

"I don't know. But it has to be a lie!"

I was almost relieved to see the police car draw up. Dad watched through the blinds. "Well, here they are back again. More publicity. Is that what you wanted all along?"

It had been when we planned it. We had giggled that day in Kilmacolm as we talked of the tv interviews we would be asked to do, the welcome, the praise. If Jude had come back when she was meant to, it would have been a heart-warming story. But she had changed the script, and I couldn't understand why.

Dad sat silent, his eyes downcast, as the police questioned me. I could see that any trust he'd had left in me was shattered.

"Judith is saying she's scared of you," the WPC said. I could hear the hostility in her tone.

"Ha, that's a lie."

"She says she didn't come back because she was afraid of you."

"Well that's a joke."

"You have got a reputation in school as a bit of a loner."

"Nobody in that school's got a good word for me now, I'm sure."

"Judith says she wanted to come back but you wouldn't let her."

"How many times do I have to say it? That's a lie."

"She was staying at your aunt's house."

"There is no way she was staying there!" My last hope was that this would be proven untrue and would show Jude up for the liar she was.

"No, it's no lie, Abbie. We've been there. We used the key you gave her."

My dad covered his head with his hands and let out a long sigh.

I was going crazy. "I didn't give her any key." I looked at Dad. "I'd never give anybody Auntie Ellen's key!"

"Then how did she get it?"

I felt like pulling my hair out by the roots. I had no answers for all of this. "I don't know. She must have made a copy."

The policeman raised an eyebrow as I said that. "She would have to get your key to do that. Did you give her the key at any time?"

"No, of course I didn't..." But my key would have been in my bag at break times, or PE, left in my locker... Could she have taken it then? It was the only explanation I could come up with.

"And she did receive several calls while she was there, from a phone box. She says they were all from you."

I almost shouted 'That's another lie!' but what was the use? They didn't believe anything I said. Jude had much the better story. She had denied sending me any texts, apart from the one begging to come home. They had already decided that the others had been sent by some of my classmates winding me up, and now I realised they were probably right.

"I never called her. How could I, when I didn't know she was there? It wasn't me." But I could tell by their cold expressions they didn't believe that either.

They left at last, still dangling the threat of charging me with wasting police time, or perhaps something worse. I couldn't get Dad to talk to me about it. He looked ready to cry. This was a man who was out marching for every lost cause there was, and if ever there was a lost cause it was me right now, but I couldn't get him to listen.

By the evening, the story of where Jude had been hiding was in the local paper, all over the Scottish news and all over social media too. Neighbours of my aunt were interviewed on tv, asked if they had seen anything suspicious. They'd noticed the lights going on in the house, they said, but my aunt had left them on timer while she was away, so they thought nothing of it.

Finally, Dad switched off the news, and put on a DVD, some old war film where everyone got killed. He needed something to cheer him up, he said. He unplugged the phone too. Because besides requests for interviews, there were so many abusive calls, calling me names, saying the awful things that should happen to me because of this, insulting me in every horrible way they could.

I was all over social media too. Someone posted that picture caught by Sara Flynn's cameraman, when I had almost flown at Jude for her lies. My eyes wide with anger, my mouth open in a roar, my face white. I looked like something out of a horror movie. They wrote under it:

Glasgow_Grl

Is this the face of evil?

257 ▣ 387 ♡ 194 ○

***

clyeboy999 commented:

Abbie Kerr #TotallyEvil

189 ♡

I didn't know how to defend myself. I lay in bed and listened to my heart hammering in my chest. I'd never felt so alone, or so afraid. Jude had been in my aunt's house, with my key. How did she manage that? What was happening?

And I still had to face tomorrow.

TWENTY-TWO

The next day was every bit as bad as I'd feared. Though no one said a word to me – and I mean not a word. I got the silent treatment. It was as if they had all got together and decided to freeze me out. They turned their backs on me, or pulled away in the corridors as if I was the carrier of some horrible disease.

Mr Madden held me back at the end of class. "Abbie, we can't make people talk to you, but we'll try to make sure nothing happens to you in school. Please report anything that does."

"Yeah, then I'll really be hated for grassing them up."

He sighed. "You're hated already. You know you are. You did a terrible thing, Abbie. They trusted you and you made a fool of them. Now you're suffering for it."

"The thing is, it wasn't just me, sir. And I'm the only one who's suffering."

"I know," was all he said. Did he believe Jude was just as much to blame as me? Did he believe she was lying? I hoped so. "It's a nine-day wonder, Abbie. Something else will happen, and it'll be forgotten. For now, the school will do its best to shield you from the worst, but you'll just have to ride out the storm."

Jude didn't have to ride out the storm though, did she? In the next couple of days word went round that she wasn't coming back to St Thomas's. She was going to another school in Greenock. I had so hoped she would come and face the music, just as I had to. But I was on my own.

Her family held a press conference, which was on tv. Sara Flynn was right up front, of course. Jude was sitting between her parents, clutching her father's hand while her mum's arm was draped around her shoulders. Her parents thanked everyone for their concern and their prayers, and said over and over how grateful they were that they had their daughter back.

Then, with lowered head and her words hardly discernible, her voice low and trembling,

Jude apologised to everyone. "I am so sorry for all the worry I caused, and I want to thank everyone, too, for being so kind and understanding to me in spite of... what I... we... did..." She never repeated the accusation against me; in fact, my name wasn't mentioned, but once had been enough. She drew in a sob and her eyes welled up with tears.

Was I the only person who could see the phoneyness behind those tears? She was acting it out!

Later, in one of those news discussion programmes, there was another item about Jude and me, and about something called 'folie a deux'. I had never heard of such a thing, didn't know what that meant, but the presenter explained it as "a madness shared by two". The medical term was 'shared psychotic disorder' – a bond between two people that brings out the worst in them. It's when two people combine, who wouldn't do anything bad on their own, but together they can do the most evil things. Like me and Jude.

Always, the presenter said, there is a dominant personality, the one who controls and manipulates the other, weaker person – the one who "leads them down that dark path." There was no question who she was assuming was the leader in this case.

That angry photo of me filled the screen. Scowling, dark eyes, grim expression. The photo they used of Jude was smiling. She was wearing a summer dress, her shiny brown hair flowing around her shoulders, her apple-red cheeks glowing. I know who I'd suspect. Not the fresh-faced teenager, but the smoky-eyed girl with the sinister look.

Did everyone think I had manipulated Jude? Ha, if only they knew. If only they believed me.

A nine-day wonder Mr Madden had said. How I prayed for those nine days to be over.

I had been warned not to try to see Jude, not to call her. So I had no chance to confront her for the truth.

The atmosphere at home was tense. Dad was civil, but that was all. He took my Auntie Ellen's key off me, muttering something about closing the stable door after the horse had bolted. That hurt. Auntie Ellen had trusted me to look after her house, and I had let her down – and I didn't even know how.

At school still no one spoke to me.

And the messages continued.

> Missing the publicity hen?

> Everyone hates you.

> Bitch Abbie Kerr

I blocked the sender as soon as they came in, but the same things got posted online and sent as text messages.

I asked Dad if I could go to a different school, like Jude.

"I live here. I work here. I moved here for my job, I've just bought this house. You've only just started in that school. So, no, Abbie, you're staying where you are."

I faced the music every day.

I was in the school library a couple of days later when one of the messages came in.

> **Tracey Mullan**
> Still not speaking to you

I was so fed up with it I sent my phone spinning across the floor. It came to a stop at Robbie's feet. I didn't expect him to even pick it up for me. But he did. He came forward and handed it to me. I held it out so he could read the message.

"That's what I'm getting all the time. How do you think that makes me feel? Do you think Jude's getting any messages like that?"

Another item about Jude had been on television the night before. Just a photo and the story. She had gone and apologised to William Creen, a private apology, and it seemed William Creen had been happy with it. "Judith Tremayne has insisted that at no point had she said she was afraid of Mr Creen." The smiling reporter said to the camera. "This was not something that came from her." The unsaid implication: it had come from me. I had wanted to run out of the house at that point, to race down the streets towards Jude's house. To tell her – to tell the world – it wasn't me who had said anything about Creen, I had only passed on a message. But I had been warned to stay away from Jude's house, hadn't I? Once again, I was the bad one.

William Creen was interviewed, happy to be cleared of all suspicion. "Of course I forgive her. It took a lot for the wee lassie to apologise like that," he said. "I don't blame *her*."

No. No one blames Jude. The *her* he blamed was me.

"You still don't realise what you've done, Abbie." Robbie broke into my thoughts.

"I do!" I snapped at him. "I apologised to the whole school. A grovelling apology, in public, and not one person said 'It took a lot for the wee lassie to do that!' Oh no. Well I am not going to apologise any more. And I'm not taking any more of these vicious messages."

"'Still not speaking'. It's not that vicious."

"You're not getting them. You don't understand. Nobody understands!" And I snatched the phone back from him. "Getting a taste of my own medicine, eh Robbie? Isn't that what you said? Well, I'm not just getting a taste of it, I'm getting it poured down my throat."

It was as I was coming out of school later that day that the phone pinged in my pocket.

I pulled it out, expecting another text saying I was totally evil. I was going to delete it. They'd soon get fed up if I just kept blocking people and didn't ever respond to their sick messages. I was going to make them sorry for a change.

Then I read it.

UNKNOWN

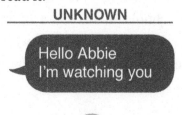

Hello Abbie
I'm watching you

TWENTY-THREE

I swivelled round. Almost everyone in the wind-whipped plaza was on their phone, either texting or messaging or calling or checking their profiles online. None of them seemed to be looking at me.

There was Andrea, chewing gum, surrounded by Belinda and Tracey, all of them with their phones clamped to their ears. There was Robbie, heading out through the main doors, typing into his phone as he walked. I saw William Creen's nephew, Josh, with his back to me. Could he be deliberately turned away, or was he just protecting himself from the wind? He was certainly tapping something into his phone. Then my eyes moved up to the first floor of the school. There was a figure at one of the windows. I couldn't make out who it was, not even whether they were a boy or a girl. It seemed to me they moved back quickly as soon as I glanced towards them. Had they been watching me as I read the text, as my eyes scanned the yard? Or was I just being paranoid?

Hello Abbie
I'm watching you

Was it a threat? Or had this UNKNOWN seen how upset everything was making me? Maybe the text was their way of letting me know I wasn't alone? But why UNKNOWN? Why not let me know who they were?

I stood in the plaza for ages. Buses left, cars drove off, the wind rose. But no one came towards me, no one even looked my way. I stood until I was alone. The grey clouds hung heavy over the hills. It would rain soon, the clouds would slash open and a deluge would pour down. And still I stood.

The entrance door to the school slid open. It was Mr Madden. I held my breath as he hurried toward me. I hadn't considered UNKNOWN might be a teacher. Yet, why not? That would account for why they were blocking any recognition of their number. A teacher wouldn't want me, a pupil, to have their mobile number. Maybe he was just letting me know he was keeping his eye out for me.

He came up close, holding his coat closed against the bitter wind.

"Are you ok, Abbie?"

I didn't answer him.

"Are you waiting for someone?"

Am I waiting for you? I wanted to ask, but the words hung in the air silently.

"Come on, I'll give you a lift home. You've missed all the buses." He gestured behind him. Mrs Speke, another English teacher, was running towards us, her long hair whipping out in the wind as if it was alive. "I'm giving Mrs Speke a lift too. We go right past your place."

At last I found my voice. "No, no. Thank you, but I'm waiting for my dad."

He nodded, patted my shoulder. "I know you're going through a hard time. I'm keeping my eye on you."

Mrs Speke caught up. She hardly acknowledged me, almost as if I wasn't there at all. And they both began to hurry to Mr Madden's car.

I'm keeping my eye on you. Almost the same as 'I'm watching you', wasn't it? Yet why did it sound so different? He was the only one who showed me any kind of sympathy. Could Mr Madden be UNKNOWN?

Over the next couple of days I waited, watched out for another text. I hated myself for being so pathetic, so desperate for some kind of contact that just might be friendly, someone trying to let me know they were there. Maybe someone a bit afraid to let the rest of the school see they were on my side. Then the next minute, I was sure it was all different. The message was sinister. I'd seen enough horror movies to know 'I'm watching you' could mean I was being stalked by some kind of serial killer. Or someone from school really trying to scare me.

Was this UNKNOWN the same one who texted *HELP ME* when Jude was away? That was a text too, not a message, and both were from UNKNOWN.

Every night my phone lay close at hand on my bedside table. I spent so much time watching it, not sure whether I wanted it to light up with a message or not. Then I'd shut it in the drawer and try to forget about it.

After a couple of days I almost managed that. I wanted to put everything behind me and move forward. The police had said that if I was going to be charged, there would be a letter from the Procurator Fiscal, but so far nothing had arrived, and with each passing day I hoped they would forget about it all too.

It was Thursday, and on Thursdays I always made a special tea for Dad, though lately we had been eating in silence. I wanted to change that. So on the way home from school I went into the supermarket to get their 'Dine In for Two' deal.

I began to feel hopeful. That day I had only had a few abusive messages and texts. Maybe Mr Madden had been right. It was a nine-day wonder.

I wandered round the aisles, picking up shampoo and milk and trying to remember what else was running low at home. The 'Dine In for Two' deal offered chicken piri piri, which Dad loved. I was at the checkout with my basket when the phone pinged. I had a text. My first thought, my hope, was that it was Dad, reminding me to pick up something nice for tea.

But it wasn't.

UNKNOWN

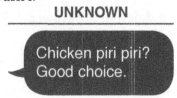

Chicken piri piri?
Good choice.

TWENTY-FOUR

I swung round. The supermarket was busy, people striding in and out of the aisles, pushing trolleys, stopping to chat, blocking my view. I was searching for a familiar face. Someone from my class, from school, someone I recognised.

"Have ye got your club card, hen?"

The voice of the girl at the checkout came through in a blur, but I couldn't answer her. My phone pinged again, urging me to look at a new text.

UNKNOWN

> Hope you enjoy that chicken.

UNKNOWN was in this supermarket, saw what I had put in my basket. Someone here was watching me.

"Hen, are you listening to me?"

The woman behind me, impatient to move, tutted. "The cashier's waiting." She nodded to the girl at the till, "We're all waiting."

But all I could think was UNKNOWN was in here. I had my chance to find who it was. I pushed past the queue, leaving everything I had chosen sitting on the conveyor belt.

The cashier shouted, "You cannae leave all that!"

I heard someone say, "That's the lassie that caused all that trouble. Kerr – was that her name?"

"So it is," someone agreed. And in seconds news of my notoriety spread like a virus through the supermarket.

I ran along the aisle where I had picked up the chicken, searching frantically for any face I recognised. I blasted into trolleys, pushed them aside; irate shoppers shouted at me. I knew I looked like someone crazy, but I couldn't explain to anyone what I was doing. No one would believe me. I was only looking for attention again, that's what they would say.

Hope you enjoy that chicken. I wanted to shove that text into someone's face, yet I knew to anyone else it wouldn't seem threatening at all. Sounded like a friend I'd met earlier in the shop, someone who'd seen me pick up the chicken and had sent me a quick text. That's what everyone would say: it must have come from a friend. That was a joke in itself. What friends did I have?

The text sounded so innocent, but it scared me.

Then I had a thought. Perhaps UNKNOWN had been at one of the other tills, waiting in a queue like me. Whoever it was would be outside now. I ran again, and stood at the entrance. It was a dark dreich day, and soon it would be darker. I hurried into the car park – maybe UNKNOWN was already in one of the cars? I ran, peering into car windows, desperately seeking a face I knew. People stared back out at me, and I could almost read their minds. Any sympathy melted when they recognised me, and realised who I was.

After a while I gave up and stood in the shelter of the trolley bay, and tried not to cry.

We didn't have our chicken dinner that night. I'd left everything on the cashier's conveyor belt. When I got home I opened a tin of chilli we had in the cupboard and Dad and I ate it with nachos.

"Did something happen today?"

I was amazed he even noticed; he had hardly spoken to me since he came in.

"I got a text when I was in the supermarket, Dad."

He let out a long sigh, fed up with the whole thing. I took my phone from my pocket and handed it to him. He glanced, and handed it back. "Doesn't sound too threatening."

"I knew you would say that, but don't you see, Dad, somebody was watching me. They saw what I put in the basket."

He tried to make light of it, and I knew he was doing it to make me feel better. A wave of love for him swept over me. I wanted to hug him. I wanted him to hug me. "Just forget about these texts, Abbie. Ignore them." Then he smiled, the first for a long time. "I would have enjoyed that chicken," he said. "Better than this blinkin' chilli."

But I couldn't smile back. He didn't understand. No one did. "That's not the first text I've had."

I scrolled to find the first one from UNKNOWN: *I'm watching you.*

And handed him back the phone.

"I thought you were deleting all these texts? Why keep this one?"

"Because it's from UNKNOWN. It's like the ones I was getting while Jude was away."

I shouldn't have mentioned that. Dad pushed the phone back at me. "Delete these as well! You can only blame yourself for all of this, Abbie. You and that so-called friend of yours."

And in that instant I knew he was right. Who had got me into all this trouble? Jude. Who had passed all the blame on to me? Jude. She'd sent the texts from a withheld number while she was gone, and I'd bet she was to blame for these texts too.

Jude was UNKNOWN.

TWENTY-FIVE

I itched to go directly to Jude's house and confront her, but I knew I had to plan carefully. I thought of sending a text to her old number, a nasty text telling her what I'd do to her if she kept on with this – and then I realised how stupid that would be. Jude would have been able to use that text against me, and then I'd be in even more trouble. My life was falling apart and all because of her (ok, maybe I was a wee bit to blame, but I didn't deserve all this). I spent that night 'nursing my wrath to keep it warm'. We'd been doing Robert Burns in school, and I remembered that line. I liked it. It sounded just the way I felt.

I didn't march straight to her house next morning, because chances were she'd already started out for her new school down in Greenock. I'd have ended up dealing with her mother, when it was Jude I had to see. I promised myself I would go at the end of the day. And I would talk to her calmly and sensibly. I would not lose my temper.

I considered running away, but had a feeling no one would come looking for me. They'd probably think it was another hoax.

Isn't it funny that even in the worst times, you still do the normal everyday things? It was morning, so I went off to school, as normal. I would get through the school day and then I would confront Jude. I had to. I had to find out if she was UNKNOWN.

It was hardly worth my while being in classes, I wasn't taking in any of it. I pressed the wrong button in I.T. and crashed the computer. All I could think about was finding out the truth from Jude. I would be calm, polite, coherent. I played the conversation over and over again in my head: what I would say to her, and what she would say to me, and in my mind she always apologised and confessed. Confessed to her lies, confessed she was UNKNOWN. In my imagination, it was all so easy.

I did manage to do a little sleuthing about where people had been the day before when I'd been trying to buy chicken. Tracey had had a fight in the school plaza and was kept in till her mum came to get her.

Robbie had stayed back with Angus in the studio, and Andrea was at drama class, so none of them could have been at the supermarket and seen me. I couldn't account for Belinda, or Josh Creen. Though I hardly suspected any of them really.

No, Jude was my chief suspect.

After school I headed for her street. I figured I'd be there before she arrived – she had further to travel to get home. I would wait for her at the corner.

All of my calm, polite intentions went out of the window when I saw her strolling along in her new uniform, giggling into her phone, flicking her hair, not a care in the world. How dare she look so happy!

She spotted me.

Her expression was worth gold. She began to babble, probably telling whoever she was speaking to that the mad Abbie Kerr was about to attack her. She was almost right.

I ran at her. "Why are you doing this to me?"

She stumbled back. "What? What are you on about?"

I pushed my phone into her face. "This! You're texting me on another phone. The one you used when you were away. UNKNOWN. It's been you all the time, admit it."

She was beginning to recover from the shock of seeing me. "Get that out of my face." She tried to push past me, but I stood my ground.

"What are you doing it for, Jude? Why not just let it be? You've won. Everybody thinks you're a saint and I'm the bad one."

She tossed back her hair. "It's not me texting you. Why would I do that?"

"Because you hate me. I don't know why. You got dumped and I tried to be a friend to you. You and me against the world, remember? What happened? How could you turn against me like that? You've got me into so much trouble with your lies."

"I didn't tell any lies," she spoke right into my face, "and you know I didn't. You're the one who should admit it."

"You did. You said it was all my idea. You said you were scared of me. You said you wanted to come back and I wouldn't let you." My voice was rising. I couldn't help it. "You said I threatened you."

Jude was the one who suddenly sounded sensible. Her voice was quiet. "I think there's something wrong with you, Abbie. I've said that to my mum. Everything I said is true and you know it, and you're either lying, or you're not admitting it to yourself. I mean, how else would I get the key to your aunt's house? You gave me it."

I didn't want to hear what she was saying. "I didn't. It's only me and you here, Jude. Tell the truth."

"You know I am telling the truth. For some reason you need attention, and this is your way of getting it." She tapped her head. "I think there's something wrong with you... up here. That's exactly what I think."

Well, no one would let that go, would they? How was I meant to keep calm after that? I grabbed her by the lapels of her brand new blazer and I rammed her up against a lamppost. Jude was bigger than me but no match when it came to fighting. "Tell the truth! Tell everybody the truth!"

I was ready to punch her but a shadow loomed behind me and an arm pulled me back. It was her mum.

"You've already been warned to stay away from here! If you ever come near Jude again I'm calling the police. I'll get a restraining order against you."

In spite of all the promises I'd made to myself, I'd managed to cause a scene in the street. Neighbours were peeking through blinds or standing at their open front doors, watching, recognising me.

Mrs Tremayne led Jude inside their house and I had to stand there, knowing all those disapproving eyes were on me. Finally I slumped away.

Why was Jude still persisting with her lies even when we were alone? Surely with me she could tell the truth?

She'd said I was lying to myself. As if that could be true. Why would I do that? Why would anyone?

Because I still need attention, she said.

Confronting Jude hadn't made anything better. In fact I had made things worse. I imagined her mother on the phone to the police, complaining about me. If she did, it might sway the Procurator Fiscal to charge me. There might even be police waiting for me at home.

I wished there was someone *I* could complain to. I couldn't talk to anyone. If my Auntie Ellen was here, I could talk to her, I could always talk to her... but when she found out Jude had been staying in her house, would she think I had really let her stay there? Would she think what everyone else did? Would she turn against me too? I had no one.

No-mates-Abbie.

TWENTY-SIX

"What's wrong wi' your face?"

I was back in the school library. I haunted it these days. It was the only place in the school I felt safe, cowering in an alcove behind stacks of shelves. I never thought the day would come when I, Abbie Kerr, would cower. I hated myself for that. I had always been a girl who swaggered. Who didn't care what anyone thought. What was happening to me?

"I said, what's wrong wi' your face?" Robbie repeated. I never knew why he was in the library. He wasn't exactly an avid reader and he didn't need to hide from anyone. "Are you ok?"

"Do you care?"

"Not particularly," he said casually. "But I was going to sit there."

"Too bad. I was here first."

"Under false pretences. You're not even reading a book. This is a library, you know."

"I'm wondering how you figured that out actually."

"At least I've got a book." He held it out to me. "Reading up about urban myths. Remember? Madden wants us to discuss urban myths and conspiracy theories for Halloween."

I vaguely remembered Mr Madden mentioning something about it, but I had hardly been concentrating.

"Are you ok?" he asked again, almost as if he meant it.

"Do you remember those texts I was getting, when Jude was still away? The ones from an unknown number?" Why was I confiding in him when I'd promised myself I'd never tell anyone about UNKNOWN? But the words were out before I could stop them, like naughty weans sneaking out at night.

"You're still getting them?"

I looked at him. There was a tiny moment in the past when I'd thought he liked me, admired me even. Did I see any of that admiration left in his eyes?

No.

"You're still getting them?" he asked again. "Is that what you're claiming now?"

If he hadn't added that 'claiming now', I might have told him. I might even have shown him the texts. But I knew he thought this was just another sad attempt to get attention. My hackles rose. I stood up and lifted my bag. "Here's a seat. You and your book need it more than me."

As I walked to class I passed Mrs Baird's office. She was the school counsellor and she had asked me several times to come and see her. I'd gone once, just for the sake of having someone listen to me. I thought she was supercilious and snobby, looking down her patronising nose at me. According to her, everything I had done was about my mum dying. I was searching for attention, she told me. I didn't like her. Didn't like the way she sat with her legs neatly crossed and her clipboard on her knee taking notes, nodding her head at everything I said, a tight smile on her face.

Yet, I hesitated at her door. I had no one else to talk to. And she would have to listen, wouldn't she? But, I wondered, did she have to take an oath like a priest or a doctor – a promise never to divulge anything she was told? Even as I thought it,

I remembered seeing her in the corridor laughing with the other teachers. What if she'd been telling them about the silly pupil with problems who came to her? Maybe she thought her oath of silence didn't stretch to children.

After a moment, I walked on.

Everyone was excited about our English lesson. It was almost Halloween: parties were being planned, costumes chosen, ghost stories were being learned to tell on sleepovers.

"Urban myths," Mr Madden began. "Who knows any?"

Daft question, I thought. Plenty of weirdos in our class love that kind of thing.

Almost every hand shot up.

Mr Madden settled himself on the edge of his desk. "Ok Robbie, what have you got?"

"Slenderman, sir," Robbie shouted. "He's brilliant."

There was a roar of approval. Everyone loved Slenderman stories. "Yep, I've heard of him," the teacher said.

"He's scary to look at, long and thin and evil and kind of faceless and pure white."

"But he's not a myth. Slenderman's real," Tracey shouted.

Mr Madden shook his head. "Totally made up, Tracey. Someone created him and put a few clips of him on YouTube, and before you knew, people were seeing him everywhere."

Tracey refused to believe that. "No sir, there are two girls in America, and they actually met him, for real, and he told them to kill somebody, and they did. They were put on trial for it."

"They might believe they met him, but you can read about the guy who made him up. Slenderman's not real. It's like a kind of mass hysteria. One person says they saw him, and before you know it, someone else claims they saw him too. That's what makes an urban myth."

"I think those two girls were just pretending they met him. They want to get publicity, to get famous," Big Belinda turned her eyes on me. "I mean, it worked for her."

"That's enough, Belinda," Mr Madden said sternly. "I think we'll move on from Slenderman."

They all waved their hands in the air, eager to tell their own urban myth.

"The babysitter, sir," Big Belinda began dramatically. "That's pure scary. Oh please, can I tell this story?"

Mr Madden smiled and nodded.

Belinda went on. "This babysitter is like... babysitting."

There was a murmur of giggles around the class. Mr Madden silenced them with a lift of his hand. "Go on, Belinda."

"Well, this night she sees they've got this big statue of a clown in the living room, and it freaks her out."

"It would freak me out too, I hate clowns." Andrea just had to butt in.

Belinda nodded sympathetically, and carried on. "So it scares her so much she covers it with a... a cover, like, so she doesn't have to look at it, like. Anyway, about midnight the parents of the wee boy, or, maybe it was a wee lassie, I'm not sure, anyway, the parents she was babysitting for, they phoned up, and asked if everything was ok and the babysitter said aye, everything was fine... because it was a really nice house they had, and they always left pizza or something for her in the fridge... and..."

I let out a long sigh. Remind me not to let her tell a story again, I was thinking.

"...except, she said, for that clown statue you've got. It is absolutely freaking me out, she said, and

I've had to cover it up, I hope you don't mind. And the parents said..." She paused for dramatic effect, looked round the class to make sure everybody was listening. "They said: We don't have a clown statue."

There was a gasp from those who hadn't heard the story before.

Belinda carried on smugly. "And this babysitter, she turned and looked at the statue and the cover began to slip from the clown's face ever so slowly..."

"Oh my goodness, I hate clowns!" someone shouted. And others called out that they did as well.

I hate clowns too – always have – something about them terrifies me, and though Belinda had told the story badly, it still sent a chill down my back.

"So, how many people here are freaked out by clowns?" Mr Madden asked. Most of the girls and some of the boys put their hands up. Without thinking about it, I put mine up too. Tracey was the first to notice.

"You, Abbie Kerr. *You're* scared of clowns?" She said it as if I had no right to be scared of anything. "I thought clowns would more likely be scared of *you*."

I pulled my hand down quickly, annoyed at myself for letting any of them in on a weakness.

"I wonder why that is? Do you think it might

have something to do with the Stephen King novel *It*?" Mr Madden asked.

Turned out half the class hadn't read the novel. Those who had read it loved it. "That was so scary, sir."

This all led to a heated discussion of why we might fear clowns. "The fear of clowns is sometimes called coulrophobia," Mr Madden told us, as he wrote the word on the whiteboard. "And it's widespread."

"Have you heard the latest about clowns, sir?" Robbie was scrolling through his phone. "I saw it on the internet last night."

"Show me."

Robbie handed the phone to him. "It's been all over YouTube, sir, and on people's newsfeeds. Clowns have been appearing everywhere: in people's gardens, at their windows. On the street."

"Oh my... Can you imagine a clown's face just appearing at your window...?" Belinda looked as if she was about to faint.

The old me would have pointed out that Belinda's face appearing at a window would be even scarier.

"Well scary. Especially if you lived on the thirteenth floor," Robbie said, and that set everyone laughing.

"I can get it up on the smartboard, sir." Andrea pushed forward to show off her tech skills. Too late: Robbie was already at Mr Madden's laptop. She didn't like that one bit – flounced back to her seat angrily.

Sure enough, between Mr Madden and Robbie a sudden image appeared on the big screen in the classroom. The figure of a clown, standing in darkness in someone's garden, sent a gasp through the whole class.

"That was in Newcastle, sir," Robbie said. "But they've been seen in Liverpool and Manchester, all over the place."

Belinda let out another dramatic cry. "They're heading west! Wonder who's next." She stared at me. "Hey, look at Kerr's face. She's chalk-white. You really are scared of clowns!"

I looked away from her quickly.

"Her face is always chalk-white," Robbie pointed out.

Mr Madden banged his fist on the desk. "That's enough. The point of this wasn't to scare anyone. Urban myths are interesting. Where they come from, how they grow. Before you know it, people begin to forget they're made up, they really believe they're real. Then everybody starts to see things that match the myth. That's what I mean about mass hysteria, Belinda. But believe me, if you see a clown in your garden, it means there's probably a circus in town."

He set us a task: to write a story creating our own urban myth. The lesson ended with the boys walking around the classroom like zombies and the girls arguing over which was worse, clowns versus Slenderman.

I left the classroom alone, and no one noticed.

TWENTY-SEVEN

Halloween wasn't going to be any fun for me. I wouldn't be invited to any parties. Everyone was talking about the costumes they were going to rent for the school Halloween disco.

Didn't seem so long ago people were eager to be my friend – I thought back to the messages and posts, all praising me. Even Andrea had called me – I had almost felt an empathy with her. Empathy... that's the right word, isn't it? We might have been able to be friends. I could remember liking it, my fifteen minutes of popularity. Well, I was having a lot more than fifteen minutes of fame now, or, what was the word? Notoriety. I took out my notebook and wrote down the word. Notorious. That's me.

I was trying to come up with a story to start an urban myth (anything but a clown), scribbling away in the school cafe, and also trying to ignore everyone and everything around me. Trying to blot out the chat and the people passing with their trays, everyone doing their best to avoid sitting at my table. The phone in my pocket made that familiar ping. I didn't want to look, but after a moment it pinged again, urging me to check it out. What now? I wondered.

It was from UNKNOWN.

I knew it would be.

The text chilled me.

UNKNOWN

> Wot U writing Abbie?

Whoever UNKNOWN was, they were here in the cafe, watching me. I must have been wrong about Jude. She was at a different school; UNKNOWN was here. I looked up quickly, my gaze moved from one to another then another. No one even seemed to be looking my way though most of them were busy on their phones. It had to be someone in this atrium.

I stared round them all. Did Tracey just look away as I caught her eye? Was that a guilty look on Andrea's face? Or had Belinda turned her back on me so I couldn't see what she was doing?

Robbie was at the bottom of the stairs, mouthing the words of a song, dancing a little as if he was listening to music on his phone – or was that a ruse and he'd just sent me a text? There was Angus alone at a table studying his phone as if he was waiting for a call. Then I looked up to the first floor. Josh Creen was leaning over the railing, his phone in his hand, and he was watching me. Always watching me. Was it him? He certainly hated me enough.

My eyes were drawn to the message again. *Wot U writing Abbie?*

I couldn't keep quiet. Who could expect me to keep quiet? I jumped to my feet and I yelled, "Ok, who is it?" I held up my phone. "Who's doing this? Sending me these texts from an unknown number. Don't be such a coward. Come on, who are you?"

They all turned to me. Some right away, others after a few moments. Andrea let out a long sigh. "Oh no, not again. Everybody's sick of listening to you."

I ran at her. "It's you, isn't it?"

Big Belinda was suddenly between us, her massive bulk protecting her friend. She swore at me. "Andrea wouldn't waste her time on you. None of us would."

I'm not a violent person – I'm not – but right at that moment I wanted to slap her. "Who's sending these texts then?" Was that really my voice, screaming the words out, echoing up through the atrium? "Who's sending me these texts? One of you must be this UNKNOWN."

"I heard a rumour you're sending them to yourself," Tracey butted in, and giggled. That was it. I was ready to floor her. But before I got a chance, a firm hand gripped me. It was Mrs Speke.

"Come with me, Abbie." Her voice was soft but the grip on my arm was firm. I couldn't shake her off.

"What are you picking on me for? I've not done anything. *They* have." I swept my arm around, including everyone in the 'they'. "Somebody here."

I was already being moved towards the lift. "We'll talk about it in the office."

I wanted to fight and scream and claw somebody's eyes out, anybody's. I struggled against her, but she kept pushing me forward. So I tried to calm myself down. It felt as if there were two people inside me: one desperately trying to walk without a fuss, and one who was screaming with anger and frustration, and both of us were trying not to cry.

When we reached the office, Mrs Baird, the school counsellor, was already there. "I heard the commotion, Abbie. I thought it would be good for us to talk."

Mr Barr sat at his desk in his swivel chair. Mrs Baird sat opposite me, looking concerned. She crossed her legs and laid her ever-present clipboard on her knee. "Everyone knows you're going through a hard time, Abbie."

"All my own fault." I smiled, but it was no smile at all. "I'm saying that to save you adding it."

Her smile became tighter. "I know you've been having some cruel pranks played on you on social media."

Why could the woman not speak English?

"I didn't make a fuss about that, did I? This is different." Surely they would give me some credit for that. "I'm making a fuss now because this is different. Somebody in this school keeps texting me from an unknown number and it's freaking me out. Look!" I let them see the latest text.

UNKNOWN

Wot U writing Abbie?

"It doesn't seem very sinister, Abbie."

"Apart from the spelling," said Mrs Speke, with a smile.

"Well what about this one?" I hadn't deleted the older ones, despite what Dad said.

UNKNOWN

> Hello Abbie
> I'm watching you

"Again, hardly threatening."

"So you would be quite happy getting texts like this?"

Mr Barr broke in. "If you haven't let the really abusive messages bother you – and there's no excuse for them, by the way – I don't understand why you're letting these texts bother you. They seem quite harmless."

How could I make them understand, and what was the point anyway?

"And Abbie, we can't have you behaving the way you did just now. That's totally out of order. I want you to spend at least some time every day with Mrs Baird. Talk through your problems."

What made them think that was going to help me? That wasn't going to deal with UNKNOWN.

I felt like screaming. But I didn't. I agreed quietly, just to get out of that office.

So I went back to class, and had to endure all the smirks and stares and titters and I ignored them all. When the bell rang I was first out of the building, opting to take the long walk home rather than sit with any of them on the bus.

I was heading down Clune Brae when my phone pinged again.

UNKNOWN

Did U have a good day?

And before I even had a chance to read it, another message popped up.

UNKNOWN

Looking 4ward 2 Halloween?

UNKNOWN

Isn't this fun Abbie?

And then another, and then another, and I knew they weren't all from the real UNKNOWN. It was all of them making a fool of me, mocking me. All of them, every one of them who had been sitting in the atrium. All sending me silly messages.

But I also knew that among them *was* the real UNKNOWN. And the real one wasn't mocking me at all. The real one was scaring me.

TWENTY-EIGHT

More came in as the evening wore on. I sat in my bedroom with my phone in my hand just waiting for them. They kept coming, and they got creepier.

UNKNOWN

I'm coming to get you.

UNKNOWN

The next knock you hear on the door will be me.

UNKNOWN

That scratching at the window is me.

> Happy Abbie?

I lost track of what was real and was supposed to be a joke. I put the phone under my pillow; I wanted to ignore it. My teeth were chattering and I was shaking. I felt as if the pulse in my neck was about to explode. I knew I was letting this UNKNOWN – whoever it was – get to me. I was becoming obsessed, waiting for the next text. Maybe I was the one who had turned a nine-day wonder into two weeks, three weeks, maybe more. If I looked at it sensibly, none of the texts were threatening, or sinister. It was all down to the way I was reading them. Reading more into them than was really there. Surely they were too deliberately scary to be taken seriously? Most of them were like the titles of teen slasher movies. No. This was someone getting back at me because of what I had done, and perhaps it was no more than I deserved. If I ignored them all, they'd get fed up and it would pass.

So I took out my phone again.

Even more texts had come in.

> Love U Abbie. Ha just kiddin

UNKNOWN

> COMING SOON ABBIE

UNKNOWN

> WAIT UP 4 ME

Hurtful, cruel, silly, but that was all. So I sat and deleted every one. No point keeping them: even if I showed them to anyone, they would only say there was nothing threatening in them. It was what the teachers had said, what even the police had said. Whoever was behind this, I was playing right into their hands by taking it so seriously.

Well, no more. I deleted every single text from UNKNOWN and I promised myself that as soon as a message appeared I would delete it at once.

When they were all gone I felt a sense of relief. Texts on a phone couldn't harm me. So, suck it up, Abbie. Don't let them get to you any more. Every time I fall, I rise, I told myself.

That night, I switched off my phone and put it in my bedside drawer. I spent too much time on it anyway. I knew what Dad said: leave your phone behind. Ignore it. Don't carry it all the time. Live your own life.

I went downstairs and by the time Dad came in from work I had the table all set and had made him mince and mash for his tea. He looked so pleased, and I could almost see a little bit of the worry he'd had about me slip from his shoulders. "That's more like my girl," he said. "I've been so worried about you, Abbie. I hope all this," he gestured around the table, cups and saucers laid there, a jug of milk, a bowl of veg, a pot of tea. "I hope this means something's changed."

"I do want things to change, Dad. I'm so sorry for everything I've done. I promise never to let you down again."

I meant every word of that.

And next day it was as if everything was going to help me keep my word. I walked into school, my head held high. And when my phone pinged with a new text (I know, why did I even take it? But I didn't want to come home to a pile of texts either) I made a show of deleting it right away. I wanted everyone watching to see me do it. And I deleted the next one, and the next.

That day I sat in the cafe alone, but for the first time I didn't feel lonely. I was scribbling away in my notebook, still working on my urban myth, when

I became aware of someone standing in front of me. I looked up. It was Frances Delaney.

"Is it true, Abbie? Have you been swamped with texts from this unknown number?"

I didn't know what to say. Was she about to confess that she was UNKNOWN? Please don't let it be Frances, I thought. She was the only one in the school I actually liked.

"That's crap!" She turned and looked round at everyone in the cafe. Her voice carried to the pupils sitting on the winding steel stairs that led up to the first floor. "Do you hear me? That's crap. Are ye all weans? I think Abbie here deserves a break. And if I hear about anybody sending her a text, it'll be me you'll have to answer to."

Frances had never been a bully. She'd never needed to be. People did what she said because they wanted to be her friend. I felt like jumping from my seat and hugging her. But I think that would have been a step too far.

She turned back to me, her voice was softer now, "You going to the school Halloween disco?"

I shook my head. It was only days away, but there was not a chance I, Abbie-no-mates-Kerr, would be going. "No," I said.

"Cause you've got nobody to go with, I suppose, eh? Well you can come with me and my mates, ok?"

"Ok." I said it completely automatically. You don't say no to Frances. Who would ever want to? But I could hardly believe my ears.

"Good," she said, flashing one of her dazzling smiles. "See you later." She walked away, giving me a backward wave of her hand.

I glanced around. Most of the pupils were deliberately not looking at me, but the ones who were didn't look happy.

No one came to sit beside me, but I didn't feel alone after that. I had the magic cloak of Frances Delaney draped around my shoulders. And it felt good.

TWENTY-NINE

The next couple of days were the best I had had since our hoax was discovered. The texts still came, but they were less frequent, and I only glanced at them then deleted them right away. Though I have to admit some were more sinister than any I had had before.

UNKNOWN

U can't escape Abbie

UNKNOWN

I'm coming

UNKNOWN

I'm still coming

Was this the real UNKNOWN? Was there actually a real UNKNOWN? I was so mixed up I was beginning to doubt it myself.

I deleted even the sinister ones. Come if you dare, I thought. Because whoever you are, I will be ready for you. You will see me striding through the school, unafraid, head high. Frances made a point of speaking to me each day, sometimes in a corridor as she would sail past with her entourage, sometimes in the school cafe, but always in places where people could see us. She wasn't over-friendly, just a few words in passing, reminding me about the Halloween disco. But those few words made such a difference.

"See that Frances," Robbie pointed out one day in class, "she's the Mother Teresa of this school. And she's made a difference to you; I can see it. You were at the end of your rope, and she threw you a lifeline."

"How poetic," I said. "I never knew you were so good with words."

So of course he couldn't just leave it at that, could he? "She's Mother Teresa, and you're Hannibal Lecter."

"If I was Hannibal Lecter, you'd be the first thing I'd eat."

But he was right about Frances. She had thrown me a lifeline. I wondered why she was being so kind. But whenever she spoke to me, I smiled, and I felt I hadn't smiled for so long. I wanted to thank her all the time, but that would have been geeky, so I usually answered her in words of one syllable or just with an idiotic smile. I never thought I would be such a wimp.

Of course some at school were still trying their best to wind me up. When news came in of a girl going missing in Renfrew, Belinda couldn't resist shouting out to me in the corridor, "Want another candlelit vigil, Abbie?"

But I walked on and ignored her.

Dad was pleased with the difference in me too. "You're getting back into the swing of things," he said, and that made me laugh. I'd never been in the swing of anything. Always the outsider. The only time I had been part of anything was when Jude disappeared and I had become the heroine who was keeping the flame alive. And that had all been a lie. I wondered sometimes what would have happened if she had come home on that night when she was supposed to. Stumbling through the crowd, lit by the flickering candles, caught on camera. We were meant to hug, and swear life-long friendship. Fame and fortune would have been ours.

So why had Jude not come back? She'd said to her mum she wanted to come back quietly, away from the publicity, the cameras. She just wanted it to be her on her own... But... Thinking back, her return could not have been more dramatic or public. Staggering up the street, in full view of an audience, neighbours stepping out of their front doors, television cameras filming her, the full glare of publicity. Nothing quiet about it.

For the first time I wondered if that had all been planned? Was Jude that devious? I had always thought her a bit silly, not too bright. So did everyone else. Maybe she wasn't as daft as she seemed. I tried to push the thought away. Maybe I would never know the truth.

I was drifting off to sleep when the security light came on in the garden outside my window. I didn't move. It would be a cat running across the grass, or leaping the fence. It was always happening. The light came on with the slightest movement; even a high wind could set it off.

But there was no wind.

A moment later the room went dark again, but only for a second. Then the light was on again. I was always telling Dad just to shut the security off completely. It was ok for him, he slept at the front of the house – the light didn't bother him. But he insisted we needed it.

I lay for another minute waiting for the room to be plunged into darkness again. But the light didn't go off.

I gave up at last and got out of bed. I drew the blinds across and looked out. Just as I did the light went out again. But again, only for a moment. The sudden blaze of it coming back on made me blink. At first I could see nothing, still half asleep. A movement caught my eye: something at the back fence, not quite in the light. Too big to be a cat. I rubbed at my eyes and peered closer.

It began to rise, and stood tall. A shape, a dark shape, all in black, and a face, and I caught my breath. I couldn't be seeing what I thought I was seeing. It couldn't be. My imagination. It had to be my imagination.

Because there, standing in the furthest corner of the garden, was a clown.

THIRTY

A clown standing in my garden? All in black, but with a white clown face and a red slash for a mouth. I put my hands over my face to try to blot it out. I was still sleeping. I must be. This was a dream, a nightmare. I was in the middle of a nightmare and when I woke up I'd be safe in my bed. Or it was a hoax, a prank, a cruel trick. Or was I seeing things? Hallucinating? Please, let any of those be true.

But when I took away my hands and opened my eyes, it was still there.

At that moment my phone pinged. I reached out to my bedside table.

UNKNOWN

Told U I'd be watching U Abbie

I began to shake once more. This was UNKNOWN – out there in my own garden. Dressed as a clown. Why a clown? Because I had confessed to being so afraid of them. I'd done that in class, they had all been there. One of them had to be UNKNOWN. I wanted to leap from my window, run outside, drag the mask from that face and reveal... Who?

I tried to clear the fog from my mind. What could I do to prove what I was seeing? Because no one would believe me. I'd take a photo! Proof positive that UNKNOWN was here, stalking me, watching me. That UNKNOWN was real. I looked down at the phone in my hand. *Told U I'd be watching U Abbie.* I'd only taken my eyes off the figure for the second it took to re-read the text, but when I glanced back, it was gone.

I had no photo. And the garden was black.

THIRTY-ONE

I hardly slept the rest of the night. I certainly didn't go back to bed. I sat curled in the chair by the window, waiting for the security light to flash on again, my phone at the ready – determined to catch him, her, it, whatever it was. In the moments I did drift off to sleep, my imagination went into overdrive. The clown haunted my dreams.

I couldn't stop trying to work it out: who was behind that mask? Who would do this? Jude only lived a few streets away from me and she knew I slept at the back of the house...

But it couldn't be Jude. She didn't know my fear of clowns. Had to be someone in class, someone who saw how pale my face was when they talked of them.

I must have dozed off eventually because I jumped awake when the alarm went off. I was still clutching the phone and my head was lying at an uncomfortable angle on my desk.

It was still dark outside. So dark, but the clocks would change in a day or two. Then darkness would come much earlier in the evening.

Should I tell Dad about the clown in the garden? That would be the sensible thing to do. But I could hear him humming down in the kitchen. He wanted things to be better, wanted to put all of this behind him, perhaps pretend it hadn't happened at all. And would he believe me? Would he think I made the whole thing up? Would anyone believe me? The answer to that was simple. No. So when he said, "You're in a daze this morning, Abbie, Everything all right?" I made myself smile. I had heard the anxiety creeping into his voice.

"Everything's A-ok, Dad," I replied.

And he smiled back, relieved.

I walked into school and studied everyone for signs of guilt. Did Tracey giggle as I walked past her? Was Robbie looking too pleased with himself about something? Did Andrea just glance at me and look away? Could UNKNOWN be Big Belinda? Josh

Creen? I caught him staring at me as I walked up the stairs to class. He looked smug, as if he knew something I didn't. But he wasn't in my class, so he wouldn't have known about the clowns.

That night I kept the lamp on, my phone clutched in my hand on camera mode, just in case. I was sure I wouldn't sleep. Instead, as soon as my head hit the pillow I was out, as if someone had switched me off. I had a great night's sleep. No nocturnal visitors, no texts, no nightmares.

Next day, Friday, was the school Halloween disco. It was all the talk. Frances made a point of coming over to make sure I was still going. I'd rather have stayed at home, especially now, but I said I would be there. "I'm not dressing up though," I told her.

"Oh come on, you'll be the only one who doesn't."

I just shrugged my shoulders. Dressing up, looking foolish, no, I couldn't bring myself to do that. She finally gave up. "Some of us are waiting behind after school to decorate the hall. Are you up for that?"

How could I say no to Frances when she was being so kind to me. "Maybe for a bit…"

"Good girl," she said. "See you later."

But in the auditorium after school as banners were pinned to the walls, and balloons were blown up, I felt even more left out. I had nothing to do. I stood by the stage feeling stupid. Everyone was looking forward to the night, except me. They were whispering and I wasn't included in any of it. Frances came out of the hall and found me trying to make a discreet exit.

"You just want to go home, don't you?"

"Is that ok?"

"Of course it is. I'm heading up to the art rooms for some more banners. I'll be going home too after that. See you tonight."

I watched as she clattered up the winding stairs in her red high heels. She disappeared down the art corridor.

Stepping out the automatic doors, I collided with Robbie coming in.

"You're looking awful happy," he said, and I realised I was smiling.

"You don't have to sound so surprised about it," I snapped back.

But he was right. I did feel happy. Maybe tonight would be a new beginning for me.

THIRTY-TWO

Dad wanted me to dress up too. "You'll be the odd one out," he said.

"No change there then," I told him. But I said it with a smile.

Still, I was more excited going out that night than I had been for a long time. And on the drive up to the school my excitement grew. There were Darth Vaders and Princess Leias galore. Sherlock Holmes, Doctor Who, Captain America, all heading for the school. Everyone seemed to be laughing; it was a cloudless night, and the sky over the hills was covered with stars. The school was lit up in celebration, and for once I was going to be part of it. I wanted to stay part of it. Put all of the past behind me, make up for what I had done that was so wrong. I didn't want to be an outsider any more.

I had never felt that more than I did that night.

Dad parked as close to the entrance as he could. When I stepped out of the car, a blast of icy wind hit my face.

"Just give me a phone and I'll come and get you."

I imagined Frances and her friends insisting I go home with them. We'd all share a taxi, or someone's mum and dad would pick us up. Maybe for once I wouldn't need a ride home with Dad. "I might go home with my friends." That didn't sound right coming out of my mouth. But I could see it pleased him. He so wanted me to fit in.

I waved as I hurried to the front doors, watching him drive off. My insides were churning. Would anyone apart from Frances even talk to me? I just wanted to keep this positive feeling alive.

But as soon as I stepped inside, I knew something had happened. Something bad. Pupils were hanging about in groups, talking in anxious tones. There was no sign of Frances. I wanted to ask someone what was wrong, but I wasn't sure anyone would tell me. I looked around and saw a girl dressed as Cleopatra. It took me a minute to realise it was Clare, one of Frances's friends. I walked towards her.

"Frances not here yet?"

She turned quickly. "You've not heard?"

Something dark inside me began to stir. "Heard what?"

"Frances is in hospital. She had an accident."

"What kind of accident?"

Clare looked up the winding stairs from the first floor. "She tripped on the stairs and fell." Clare was almost crying. "Typical Frances. Always doing something nice for people. She stays behind to help, and this happens."

"Is she ok?"

Clare swallowed a lump in her throat. "One of the teachers is going to make an announcement in a minute."

"How did it happen?"

"Those blinkin' high heels of hers, I think."

At that point I just wanted to go home. If there was no Frances, there would be no me. I couldn't handle tonight without her. But I decided to wait for the teacher's announcement.

I could hear everyone whispering and talking about Frances.

"It's so not fair. She's so nice. I've never heard her being mean to anybody."

"I hope she's ok. I hope nothing's wrong with her legs. She's got lovely legs."

"She told me I had lovely legs as well. Me!" This was Big Belinda. Legs like tree trunks. Which shows how nice Frances is.

There, in those few words, was why everyone liked Frances. You couldn't help but like her. She complimented everyone; she always looked for someone's good points then pointed them out. She made everyone feel special.

Why couldn't I be like her? Why couldn't I see the good in people? Maybe if I complimented people more they would like me. I was always insulting Robbie, always ready with a snappy comment about everybody else.

The auditorium looked different that night. So much bigger for a start. The seats had been folded back against the wall and that made the floor seem huge. A glitter ball turned on the ceiling sending dazzling stars dancing all round the walls. There were banners pinned up and balloons and the screen was rolled down displaying music videos, plus the message:

PREPARE TO BE AFRAID!
SPILLS AND THRILLS ALL
THROUGH THE NIGHT

I felt out of place wandering into the auditorium. The only one not dressed up. But I wanted to hear what was happening for Frances. I imagined her tumbling down those steel spiral stairs, head over heels, down and down, and I felt sick. Please let her be ok, I prayed.

I felt sorry for my dad. Tonight was totally not going to work, and he had really wanted to believe life was going to be happier for me. Maybe I just wasn't the type to be happy. Every time I thought things were getting better, something happened to make it all fall apart again. Just my luck Frances managed to trip down the stairs the night of the disco. (See what I mean about me not being a nice person? Even now, I couldn't think about something going wrong for someone else without getting concerned about how it affected me.)

I felt as if I was in a little bubble separate from everyone else. Watching everything, but not really a part of it. I stood against the wall, close to the exit door, trying to merge into the background, and I watched everything that was going on. There was Andrea, dressed up as Cleopatra, watching Clare. She had an annoyed little look on her face. Two Cleopatras, and she didn't look half as good as Clare.

She saw me watching her and whispered something to Belinda, who let out one of her big, daft laughs. (See, I do not find the good in people. I could never be like Frances.) And there was Robbie, a dashing, yes, I have to admit it, a dashing pirate.

Then the music stopped abruptly. Mr Madden stepped onto the stage and turned on the microphone. We all knew he was going to make an announcement about Frances. He held up his hand for quiet, though there was no need. Everyone had stopped dancing, stopped talking.

"I just wanted to give you an update on Frances Delaney. For those of you who don't know, Frances had an accident on the stairs today. She slipped and fell and is in A&E being treated for a broken leg and several bruises. But I've just come from there, and she is comfortable and – typically of Frances – wants everyone to have a wonderful night."

There was a rousing cheer, and hip-hip-hoorays for Frances.

As Mr Madden left the stage, he was swarmed with pupils wanting more information. His eyes swept the hall but seemed to miss me entirely.

I hadn't noticed Belinda sneaking up to my side. She had the most sneering smile on her face. "Poor

Frances. Seems it's the kiss of death to try to be your friend, Abbie Kerr." Then she just walked off. I felt as if she had sunk a knife into my back.

All around me there was laughing and dancing, and I was the invisible outsider. It was never going to be all right. The only one who had been kind to me was lying in a hospital bed. I brought bad luck on everyone.

The big screen was now showing flickering images of some YouTube Halloween video, the music was loud, the glitter ball looked as if it was alive as it turned on the ceiling sending dancing shards of lights along the walls. My eyes followed them and were caught by a movement in the window of the projection room, high up on the back wall.

The room was in darkness, but I was sure I could see something in there, standing deep in the shadows, so deep it took me a moment to see it more clearly. Then it moved again, and I could make out exactly what it was.

A clown.

THIRTY-THREE

My knees trembled. I looked around the auditorium. No one else was looking towards the projection room. If they did, would they see the clown too? Had I imagined it? Maybe I'd look again and it would be gone. My eyes moved slowly, reluctantly back, and it was still there. Still lurking in the shadows. Not just any clown. I was sure it was the exact same clown I had seen in my garden. I could almost have been watching a disembodied head floating in the deep dark of the room. All I could make out was that same white face and the same sinister red slash of a smile.

UNKNOWN was back. Here. Just for me, waiting in the dark. I prayed it couldn't be real. My insides melted, my legs felt like rubber. Who was doing this to me? I looked around, wanted someone else to see it, but they were all dancing; their eyes were on the dj. And if I screamed – I so wanted to scream – they would look up to the projection room, and I knew what would happen. It would be gone. And I would look a fool, or worse, and no one would believe me. No one ever believed me.

I had no choice. I had to go up there and confront whoever it was.

I edged along the stage, moving slowly. Afraid it was watching me. I wanted it to stay there. I headed towards the door, winding my way through the crowds. At last I was outside the auditorium, and it was only then that I began to run. The door swung closed behind me and the music faded; it suddenly seemed to be coming from some far-off place. There was no one around. The projection room was at the top of a flight of long stairs leading from the bottom corridor. I pulled open the stair door and took the steps two at a time, glad my shoes made no sound on the stone. I only had one thought. I was going to find out who this clown was, who was behind the mask, and why they were frightening me.

There was a second as I reached the final door when I hesitated, fear holding me from bursting in. What if the room was empty? What if it was gone, or –worse – had never been here? What if it had heard my steps, soft as they were, and knew I was coming, and now it was waiting for me behind the door, ready to attack me? Pull yourself together, Abbie, I told myself, this is your chance to find out the truth! And I threw open the door.

It was still there. Still standing back in the shadows of the room. It didn't even turn as I came in. I didn't give it any time to turn now. I ran at it, and began beating my fists against its chest, and someone was screaming, and I knew it was me: "Who are you? Why are you doing this?!"

At the same moment, the lights in the auditorium went out, the music stopped. There was silence all around and an eerie green light was switched on in the projection room. What was happening? Were they all a part of it? But that didn't matter now. Now I could find out the truth.

I reached up and tore off the mask: "Now I'll see who you are!"

It was Josh Creen.

THIRTY-FOUR

I didn't tell Dad anything about what had happened. I made the excuse when I came home early that I'd felt awkward about not dressing up, and he was shocked when I told him about Frances, but it helped him understand why I hadn't wanted to stay. Everyone had been so nice and friendly, I told him without a blush. And Frances's friends hadn't wanted me to leave, I said brightly. All lies I wanted to be true.

I could tell he believed every word. When did I get so good at telling lies?

But how could I have told him the truth? That I had made a complete fool of myself. In front of the whole school.

SPILLS AND THRILLS they had promised, and the creepy clown appearing in the dark corner of the projection room was one of them. Not meant to scare me at all. Just entertainment at the disco. I'd looked like a fool, screaming that the clown was stalking me. That everyone was against me. That this clown had been in my garden trying to scare me.

"Me?" Josh had said. "I wouldn't waste any time on you. I don't know anybody who would."

It got worse. Turned out the microphones in the projection room were on and everyone in the auditorium was hearing every word.

They all yelled and shouted, stamping their feet, whistling and laughing – laughing at me. Here was Abbie again, looking for attention.

I had run then, trying to blot out their laughter. I ran home and smiled and lied and went to bed and cried and promised myself I would never go back to that school.

I was drifting into an uneasy sleep when my phone pinged again. Another text. I didn't want to look at it, I wanted to delete it right away, but it isn't easy. In fact, for me, now, it was impossible.

UNKNOWN

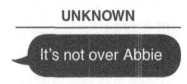
It's not over Abbie

It's not over. It would never be over. Not until I found out who was doing this.

It so wasn't fair that I was facing it all on my own. Jude had been just as much to blame but she was in another school. None of this was happening to her. Or was it? Was she getting texts like this too? Was she as afraid as I was?

Dad seemed a bit happier at breakfast. Sitting reading the paper, coffee in hand, humming to himself. "I'm so glad you enjoyed that disco, Abbie. You get yourself involved in more things at school. You'll see how things will change."

If only he knew the truth.

I heard the phone ring in the hall, and stood up to get it, but Dad motioned me to sit.

"I'm just about finished. You get your breakfast. Maybe it's for you," he smiled. "One of your friends..." he added. And I almost had to laugh. When was the phone ever for me? Unless it was a journalist wanting to say something horrible about me.

I heard him muttering away but hardly listened, my mind on so many other things. And then his voice began to rise. He sounded apologetic and embarrassed. I jumped up and pulled open the door. By that time he was putting the phone down.

He stood for a while looking at it, then turned to stare at me as if I was a stranger.

"What happened, Dad? Was that union stuff?"

"So you had a lovely time, Abbie? Everyone was so friendly. You forgot to mention you just about ruined the disco for everyone." He took a step towards me and I stepped back.

"Who was that?" I could hear my voice shaking.

"The dad of one of your so-called friends. He says you scared his daughter to bits last night with your stupid carry-on about some clown. He says he's not putting up with any more of it. He's going to have something done about you. Come Monday you are in big trouble."

"Who's his daughter?"

Dad waved that away. "Does it matter? Take your pick."

"But Dad, I didn't... I thought..." How could I explain it? I couldn't find the words. "I didn't mean..."

"You never mean anything, Abbie. What's got into you? You sat there and lied to me. I don't even know you any more."

He was right, I had lied to him, but I had had enough too. I shouted back at him, "No, you don't know me! Why should you? You're more interested in your union – that always comes first. Not me. Never me. I hate you."

"Hate me then. I've got to get out of here. I'm sick of this so much."

He was sick of it? What did he have to be sick of? "Not as sick of it as I am!" And I slammed back to my room. I waited, hoping he might come up, knock on my door, all apologies. But a half hour later, he was gone. I heard his car start up and I ran through into his bedroom, stood at the window and watched him go. I sat on his bed, hugging my knees; I was shaking. I knew there was something wrong with me, and I had nobody to help, nobody to talk to. Nobody who would understand. I sat there while a dark morning became a darker afternoon, my mind racing around like a hamster on a wheel, going nowhere.

There was a ping. The only person who ever tried to reach me was UNKNOWN.

UNKNOWN

Poor Abbie all alone. It's nearly over now.

But I shouldn't be all alone. Jude should be going through this too. She should be going through something.

I was desperate. Desperate enough even to risk bumping into her parents. I was going to go back and see Jude.

THIRTY-FIVE

It was a miserable dark and dreich November Saturday, with that drizzly rain that soaks right through to your bones. A fine mist was rising from the river. I stood at the end of Jude's street under a clump of trees that seemed determined to make me even more wet. I was trying to pluck up the courage to go to her door. I had to ask if any weird things were happening to her. I was hoping the answer was yes. Had she received any texts? Seen strange figures in her garden? Did she know why any of this was going on?

I was just about to approach the house, when their front door opened and Jude's mum and then her dad came out. Jude was with them, but in her dressing gown, obviously there just to see them away. She handed over an umbrella they must have forgotten and Mrs Tremayne pecked at her cheek. Jude went back in. I waited until the car turned the corner before I hurried up to the front door.

She must have thought it was her mother again, that they'd forgotten something else, because she pulled the door wide with a half-smile on her face. It disappeared when she saw it was me. "What do you want?" she snapped. She had her phone clamped to her ear. "Abbie," she added.

"Just listen. I have to talk to you, Jude. Terrible things are happening to me. Terrible things. And I need to know if anything bad is happening to you? I want to know if you've seen anything strange, if you're getting any strange text messages?"

"Nothing's happening to me." She tried to push the door shut, but I held it open.

"So why are things happening to me, Jude? We were in this together, so why me and not you? This is a mystery, Jude, you have to see that, and I think together we could solve it."

"There isn't any mystery. It's over. It was over when I came back. You're the one keeping it going."

"Someone's not letting it be over for me. I need to talk to you."

"Can you not see I'm on the phone?" She tried

again to shut the door, but I shoved my foot inside. Whoever was on the other end of the phone was hearing my pleas, but I couldn't stop now.

"Let me in, Jude."

Whoever she was on the phone to was still talking. Jude let out an exasperated sigh. "Oh, ok," she said, still with the phone to her ear. "You can come in. But only for a minute." She pushed open the door of the living room to let me through, but she stayed in the hall and pulled the door closed so I wouldn't hear her phone conversation. A moment later she came in, still holding her phone, but looking at me.

I pulled down the hood of my jacket. "It's not just the texts, Jude. Something was in my garden the other night."

"Really? What?"

"A clown," I said, watching her face.

She just looked as though I was strange. "That seems very unlikely, Abbie. Or maybe it was just someone on the way to a Halloween party. Or someone playing a joke." She was calm, dismissive.

Inside, I was the very opposite of calm. "I can't take much more of this, Jude. My dad and me had a terrible fight this morning. He just walked out. I said something awful. But I am getting scared.

I don't know what's going on. Honest, Jude, I'm at the end of my rope. And your life is completely normal? How is that?"

She tapped her head. "There is something really wrong with you, Abbie. You should see a doctor. You started all this, and how you got me into it, I don't know."

"I got you into this!" Did she really believe her own lies? "No I did not. You came to me with the idea, remember? Remember Kilmacolm?"

"Be honest with yourself, Abbie. I was vulnerable. And you used me. It was all your plan, and I fell in with it."

I was shaking my head. "No! We're on our own now. Why would you lie?"

"Abbie, how did I get your auntie's key? I'll tell you how. You gave it to me. You were the one told me to stay there."

"Lies, that's all lies."

"So how did I know to stay there? Talk sense. And if you are getting strange texts, well, I find the whole thing hard to believe. It's easy to send yourself a text, Abbie. And who else saw this clown in your garden, Abbie? Anyone else?"

"But it was there."

She shrugged her shoulders. "Do you know what, Abbie? I heard more today about what's happening to you. Frances is saying there was something stretched across the stairs at school to trip her up... Her fall was no accident. And you know what else they're saying...? You were the last one who saw her."

I was so shocked I couldn't even speak for a moment. "What do you mean? Nobody would say I'd do anything to Frances."

"Think about it, Abbie. It's the only logical answer. You know it is. There isn't anybody else. Nobody's threatened you. You sent those texts to yourself. There was no clown in the garden. There is no UNKNOWN, there's only you. You, Abbie, you are UNKNOWN."

THIRTY-SIX

I shook my head. I wouldn't believe that.

And still she went on. "There was no clown. You made that up. And you gave me your auntie's key. It's always been just you. Why can't you get that through your head?"

"That's stupid. Why… why would I do that?"

"Because… there's something wrong with you." She twirled her finger round the side of her head. "Up here. I've known it for a long time, that's why I was afraid of you, Abbie."

I was already backing away from her, couldn't listen any more. Just shaking my head, trying to shake out the very notion of it.

I was on the path and hadn't a single memory of leaving the house, or being pushed out. What Jude had said had floored me.

"No… no…"

I wanted to beg her, to plead with her. Wanted her to tell me she was making all of this up. I was afraid.

"If you had any sense, instead of sending yourself a text saying it's not over, you should send one saying it is. And then you could move on. If you had any sense. But then, you don't have a lot of sense, do you?"

She slammed the front door closed and I stood in the rain. One part of me was sure what she said wasn't true. But the thought just wouldn't lie down. Could she be right? Maybe they were all right. Maybe there was something wrong with me. Maybe it *was* me who made Jude leave, made her run away. Maybe it had been my plan all along. She had neither the intelligence nor the nerve to come up with such a plan, everyone said so.

And how would she have been able to get the key to my Auntie Ellen's house, unless I had given it to her, along with permission? Or had I insisted she stay there?

What other answer was there?

I had tried to deny all of this, even to myself.

I was sending these texts to myself. Had to be the answer. I had been the one in the supermarket.

The only one. Hadn't I searched in every aisle, in every car and found no one I recognised? Only me.

All these texts from someone who knew just what I was doing. Who knew but me? Why would anyone else bother with texts like that? No one would.

And there had been no clown in the garden. The talk in class had put the idea into my head.

And it had stayed in my head.

All my mad imagination.

And Frances... The last I had seen her, she was clip-clopping up the stairs in those mad high heels of hers. I had watched her. And watched her. The next moment I bumped into Robbie and he said I looked happy. Was that because I had run up the stairs after Frances and stretched something across in the hope she would trip and fall? Could I be that devious, and not remember?

When I looked at everything like that, it all fitted. The only answer: I was UNKNOWN.

And that could only mean I was mad. Crazy. They would lock me up and throw away the key. And I couldn't blame them; I needed help. I had no one to confide in, no friends, no one who even liked me.

I didn't even have Dad any more.

I crossed the street to the walkway beside the river. There was no one about on this miserable afternoon. I stood leaning over the steel railings looking out over the water. I was so mixed up. The waves lapped on the shore, and the water, even as grey as steel, looked inviting. I could slip under the railings and with only a few steps I could just wade deeper and deeper into the Clyde. The thought didn't sound frightening at all. I could almost feel the cold water lap over my head. The world would be silent down there. I could drift off with the tide and be lost forever. No one could reach me. No one could hurt me. I could just disappear forever. My troubles would be over.

THIRTY-SEVEN

It was another text that stopped me. I felt the phone vibrate in my pocket and at first I was afraid to look, terrified it would be from UNKNOWN again, urging me to take that final step. And terrified that UNKNOWN would be me.

But it was from Dad.

Dad

> Sorry bout the fight. We need to talk. Meet me at 5 at Ferguzons shipyard. Pick you up at the roundabout.

He hadn't deserted me. Dad still loved me. I knew he did. He'd been angry when he stormed out of the house, but he'd thought about it, and now he wanted to talk. And I so needed to talk to him.

I sent him a text back. I wanted to write *I love you Dad. Things are going to be better. I have so much I need to talk about... I think I know what's wrong with me.*

But all that didn't sound like me at all. He'd think he sent the text to the wrong number.

So I merely typed in ok and left it at that.

It was after four o'clock now. No time to go home and change into a dry jacket. It would take me almost half an hour to make my way along the shore, through Coronation Park, past the fire station, and be at the roundabout by five. He might suggest going out for dinner, and I loved it when we did that. Langbank was only a ten-minute drive from the roundabout, and there was a lovely restaurant there where we could sit looking out over the river to Dumbarton Rock and all the lights across the water.

I was going to be honest with him, because I was so scared. I needed to ask if he thought I had been the one doing this all along. Had he been afraid of that too? I was soaked through but now I didn't even mind the rain. I could think of nothing but meeting Dad. The dark day seemed to match my mood. An eerie mist hovered over the town, drifting ghostlike between the bare branches of trees. As I walked, I went over what I would say to Dad. I would tell him everything Jude had said, and if he thought I needed help, then I would do whatever he thought was best.

There was building work going on all round the shipyard. I knew Dad was sometimes there for the union talking to the workers. Right now, though, it was the weekend and no one was on site. Debris and bricks lay where part of the old building had been demolished. Dumpsters and forklift trucks sat as if they had been abandoned. Corrugated-iron buildings were rising on the other side of the shipyard, cut off by steel fencing and warning signs. Danger. Keep Out.

I stood sheltering as best I could, waiting, watching the cars as they drove round the roundabout heading into Greenock or up to Glasgow. I was right across from the loft apartments, a big red-brick building that used to be the Ropeworks, Dad had told me. The lights were on, I could see inside. People making meals, getting dressed for their Saturday night out, people with no worries. Not like me. Dad was late.

I stepped back further to see if I could get a view of Newark Castle, but it was blocked completely by the building work. Traffic was light. The whole area was deserted. I was alone.

My phone pinged and my heart jumped at the sound.

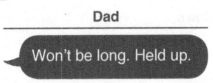

Dad

Won't be long. Held up.

Hurry up, Dad, I thought.

In the few minutes I waited, it grew darker.

There was a movement behind one of the corrugated iron buildings. Just for a second. I was sure I had seen something: a shadow, a figure. My imagination, I told myself. It was this mist coming in from the river. It was the looming darkness. I wouldn't look. I'd turn away. Because there was nothing there. It was all in my head. I was breathing faster, felt my lips go dry. Hurry up, Dad.

Anyway, even if there really was something there, it would just be boys playing around, or vandals. Or perhaps security. Or a tourist.

Or nothing at all.

Hurry up, Dad.

Another movement caught at the side of my vision, and I couldn't help it. Couldn't stop myself. I looked.

A face peeking round a steel pillar, a white face, with a red slash of a smile.

The clown.

THIRTY-EIGHT

Was it real? Was it only in my imagination? I began to shake.

The face was gone again, yet it seemed something was still there. It was too dark to see. Why couldn't I run? Dad would be here soon. I'd tell him. I'd show him. If it was real, he would see it too. But what if it was gone by then, disappeared again? What if it wasn't there at all? Something inside me needed desperately to find out what was real and what wasn't.

I blinked and there was the black figure moving against the darkness, with that face floating in the air, peering round at me. Daring me to come. Gone again in an instant. I had to see, I had to know. Without even realising what I was doing, I moved towards it.

The steel from the fencing bit into my fingers as I pulled it aside to step through. My mind was in a whirl, the pulse in my neck racing. How could I prove it was real? Was there a way? And I remembered my phone. I could take a photograph. I took the phone out of my pocket and held it tight. This time I would definitely take a photo, surely then I could prove to everyone, to myself especially, that this was real. That I hadn't made it up. And if the photograph was nothing but steel and mist, then I would know that I really was mad.

The building was just a shell, but it had a roof and steel beams running across the high ceiling. Huge steel pillars were still being inserted. I moved further inside, out of the rain at least.

"Where are you?" I yelled, hoping for an answer.

But there was nothing. I stepped over pipes and rubble. Watching for that face to suddenly appear. Where could it have hidden? But there was nowhere for anyone to hide here, and Jude's words shouted inside my head: "There's only you. You, Abbie, you are UNKNOWN."

Couldn't be real, could it? I had to get out of here. It was suddenly too dark. The sound of a movement behind me made me jump. The soft pad of a footstep close behind. And was that the breeze, or was it someone's icy breath against my hair? I swung round sharply.

I wasn't prepared. Though I should have been. Because as I turned, there it was, too close, far too close, that smile like a streak of blood. It had to be real. I wanted to scream. It was there. The clown, the white face, too close against my own.

Wisps of mist seemed to have followed it inside the building like something out of a nightmare world. I took a step back and felt my foot slip. Who are you? I wanted to ask. Couldn't say a word. I was losing my balance, had nothing to grip on to. I heard someone scream. I think it was me. I was going down, down, tumbling, nothing to hold on to. Nothing to stop me.

And then I hit the ground and blacked out.

THIRTY-NINE

How long have I been unconscious? I don't know.
When I come to, I feel groggy, my head aches. I
don't know where I am... How did I get here? And
where exactly is... here? It is pitch black now. I
can see no sky. I ache in every bone. Drip, drip,
dripping all around me. I have that feeling, as if
you've been dreaming, you're in the middle of a
terrible nightmare and then you realise it wasn't
a nightmare at all. It has actually happened.
I remember the mist. I was running after
something, someone... Then I remember the
face, that white face with the terrifying smile.
The clown. I begin to breathe faster. Is the clown
in here, in the darkness with me? I am so afraid
to turn my head in case that face is there.

Please don't let that face be behind me.

Try to think. Try to think. The fall. I had tumbled back because I saw that face in the shadows, too close to my own. If I can just think straight, it will all come back to me. Think, Abbie. My mind is muddled. The memory will not come.

I had been waiting for someone... But I can't remember who. And then I was running.

I let out a scream as I felt an ice-cold drip hit my face. Another drip. I scream again. I shout for help.

And I wait.

No one comes. I'd had a phone. Where is it? I fumble in my pockets but there is no phone. Had I held it in my hands? Had I dropped it? Had the clown taken it?

And then another memory bursts to the surface like a shark leaping from the water.

There was no clown. There never had been a clown. There is only me. And if there was no clown, there was no UNKNOWN. It all comes back. It had all been me, sending the texts, imagining the figure in the garden. After all, who else had seen it? Only me.

UNKNOWN and the clown, one and the same. Me.

Faces flit in front of me, accusing faces. Robbie and Tracey and Andrea and Josh Creen and Belinda and Frances and Jude and her mother and father and William Creen. I had wronged all of them.

But the memories are all jumbled up.

Everyone is right about me. There is something evil in me, something bad, something wrong. That's why I have no friends.

And then another horrific thought. Am I dead? Am I dead and waiting here in this dark place?

Do you feel pain when you're dead? Every part of my body aches. My back, my knees, and my ankle throbs. I'm sure it's broken. If I feel pain, I can't be dead, can I? And this can't really be hell? I'm not bad enough to go to hell, surely. I haven't killed anyone...

You've hurt people, Abbie. I can almost hear the voice of my conscience whispering in my ear.

I want to slam my hands against the walls, just to get that voice to shut up. Because it is right. I have hurt people. And here is my punishment. Trapped in a dark place, alone.

Afraid. What if no one comes back for me?

What if *it* comes back?

What if...

I start screaming, and this time I can't stop. No one knows I am here. And my screaming alerts no one. I begin to panic.

Calm down, Abbie. Breathe in, slowly. If I panic now, let my fear take over, I'll go mad. If I am not mad already. I have to do something to calm myself down. What can I do?

And it comes to me.

I will go back over everything, right from the very start, and it will calm me and stop me panicking. And maybe help me understand how I have come to this.

How did it all begin?

FORTY

 Greater Glasgow Police

Appeal for Information: Missing Teen – Port Glasgow area

Police Scotland are appealing for information to help trace a fourteen-year-old girl. Judith Tremayne is missing from her home in Port Glasgow. She was last seen on Friday around 18.00.

Judith is described as tall for her age, with long brown hair and brown eyes. She was last seen wearing a green jacket, a t-shirt and blue jeans. Her parents have said it is completely out of character for Judith not to be in contact with them or her friends. Officers are becoming increasingly concerned for her welfare.

That was how it began... or seemed to begin. For me and Jude it began weeks before on the day I found her in the girls' toilets sobbing her heart out. I'd never had much time for her, or the bunch of friends she hung about with, and she had no time for me either. But it seemed weird not to ask her what was wrong. I hadn't expected her to pour out her heart. Telling me how she'd been dumped by Tracey and Belinda and Andrea, drummed out of the gang. She had no friends now.

And I had laughed. I can still see her looking up at me when I did that. "You think that's funny?"

"You're crying over them? A bunch of losers. Andrea Glass – who needs friends like that?"

"But they were my very best friends."

"Clearly not, when they could dump you just like that." That only made her cry harder. I was saying all the wrong things. Why hadn't I gone into the toilets on the other floor? I hadn't realised that small decision would change my life. "Look, all I'm saying is, I would never let anybody get to me like that. And for a boring loser like Andrea? Grow a backbone, Jude, I'd never let anyone break me. Who cares if nobody talks to you? Nobody talks to me and it doesn't bother me."

"You don't understand. Hardly anybody likes you anyway."

"Thanks for that," I said. "No. I don't understand. No matter what they did. I'm a very strong person and I would never let anybody get to me like that. Certainly not losers like that lot. Nobody would ever break me."

I managed to make that my parting shot, and I thought it was over, until I got a call from Jude just a couple of days later, thanking me for making her feel better. That was a first, me making anyone feel better. And then, next day, there was another call and then another and then...

I should never have listened to Jude. I don't normally listen to anyone, but at that time she seemed to be in the same place as me. She was bitter about being dumped, fed up with her mum and dad. I suppose I was bitter too. We had left Glasgow to move here, and now Dad never seemed to be home, I had no friends at school. I can look back now and see I didn't deserve friends. I was arrogant and aloof and Jude's plan seemed like a good hoax. A great joke, a bit of fun that would harm no one.

"Could we get away with it?" I started asking her, and I suppose that was when I realised I was not only thinking about it, I had decided to do it.

"Who would ever know?" was her answer. She was the one who'd go missing, she said, because she knew the town better, knew places to hide. I would be the one who'd stay at home, be the heroine. What a great joke. But the joke was always on me. From the very beginning Jude must have had a plan to trick me, and I had fallen for it.

Jude had known what she was doing. But why? If she'd appeared during the candlelit vigil, fame and fortune awaited us both. She would be the prodigal child, and I would be a heroine.

But that hadn't been the plan, not the real plan. The real plan was to hurt me. That was the only answer. But why? What had I ever done to deserve all this?

I remembered the day Jude had come home. Hadn't I thought it was like a scene from a movie? Her return captured on tv cameras and recorded by all the neighbours, dramatic, full of emotion, played over and over on the news, on YouTube. Exactly as we had planned it. Only this time I was the villain.

"The only person I've ever been afraid of... is YOU!"

She had appeared at exactly the right time, just as the cameras were on her doorstep.

Very convenient.

Too convenient.

All part of her plan, stumbling into view, falling into her mother's arms. Hollywood couldn't have staged it better. All fake. All deliberate.

But why?

●●●

I've been screaming so loud my throat hurts and still no one hears me. I'm afraid to scream now. What if no one ever comes?

If only I could climb out, but there's nothing to hold onto, nothing to grip. How long will I be down here? I begin to shake.

I'm trying not to panic.

But what if nobody ever finds me?

Can't think like that or I'll go mad.

No, I will be saved. Hold onto that thought.

Someone will find me.

Someone has to.

FORTY-ONE

I think I've been asleep... or maybe I fainted. My ankle hurts so much. I'm very thirsty. If only it wasn't so dark.

Stop thinking like this, Abbie. Where were you? Go back, go back... Calm down... Going back over everything will take your mind off where you are, at least for a while.

●●●

So if that part is true, and Jude deliberately came back in full view of the camera, if that was done deliberately as some kind of punishment for me, then maybe my punishment continued after she came home. If that really happened, maybe the rest is real too. I did get those texts. I did see a clown. There was an UNKNOWN. And it isn't me.

If it is all real, then Jude is the prime suspect. But how did she get my aunt's key? If someone had wanted the key, it wouldn't have been very hard. I leave my rucksack in the changing rooms, and in my locker sometimes. And I never lock my locker door, hardly anyone does. Perhaps Jude took it, had a copy made. Must have, only solution.

But wait a minute... UNKNOWN. Jude hadn't been there in school when I got the text in the cafe. How could she have known I was writing?

And I had hardly seen Jude since. So maybe UNKNOWN had nothing to do with Jude, maybe Jude's part had ended with her return. UNKNOWN was payback for all the terrible hurt I'd caused. Someone afterwards who wanted to make me suffer, make me realise what I had done.

What was it Robbie had said? "You need a taste of your own medicine." Was this Robbie's way of telling me that he is UNKNOWN? He could be. He's the I.T. expert, he's smart, and I could imagine him dressing up as the clown to scare me.

But to be so cruel?

Or Josh Creen? Despite what he said at the disco, he hates me, and I know he's been watching me.

●●●

I drift off into a nightmare sleep. Images flash across my mind: Robbie, with a cruel smile on his face, whispering, "You need a taste of your own medicine."

Josh Creen taking off a clown's mask and saying, "You'll get what's coming to you."

And then Sara Flynn, smiling and pushing a camera into my face. "Have you seen the television, Abbie? The answer's there."

Whispers, so many whispers, if I could just make out what they were saying. Texts flicking past. I can't quite read them.

●●●

My dad's text slaps in front of me, like a paper blown against a window.

Dad

> Sorry bout the fight. We need to talk. Meet me at 5 at Ferguzons shipyard. Pick you up at the roundabout.

And it is all nagging at my brain. Something here in this nightmare I just can't quite grasp... What is it? The answer, Sara Flynn says. The answer was on tv. What was on tv?

I jump awake. Am I just clutching at straws? Is the answer really in my dream?

I so need to go to the toilet. I get to my feet and I can hardly stand. Can't put any weight on my ankle. My legs are shaking. I'll go in the corner but the corner is so dark.

•••

My dad will be worried about me. My dad! I remember again the text he sent me, as clear as it was in the dream. I was supposed to meet him. That's why I came to the shipyard. When he'd come and seen I wasn't waiting, he would have known something was wrong. He'll have people searching all round here.

My dad! Anytime now he'll come, help will arrive. Just thinking that makes my breathing come easier.

It was a cruel plan Jude and I came up with, it hurt too many people. At least I've learned that. But is being sorry enough?

I fall asleep again. Didn't mean to, and when I wake up it's not so dark. I can see some light, what time is it, what day is it? Is it Sunday? Why hasn't Dad come with help?

Because it wasn't Dad texting you, Abbie.

And the realisation makes me cry.

Of course it wasn't Dad. UNKNOWN is clever. UNKNOWN could figure out how to grab Dad's phone and send a message. He's always leaving it on his car seat, on tables, in his jacket. That text got me here to this lonely place, and then... A brief glimpse of the clown did the rest.

Another nagging feeling.

Something I should have noticed but I can't grasp it.

Then it hits me. Whoever wrote that message knew I'd fallen out with my dad. And the only person I told was Jude. And something else Jude said: "You shouldn't send a text saying, *this isn't over...*" But I hadn't mentioned that text, hadn't shown it to anyone. The only way she could have known about it was if she'd sent it.

I keep coming back to Jude. She has to be UNKNOWN.

I'm so cold. Can't stop shivering.

I know now that Dad won't come. I wonder what he thinks. That I've run away after the fight? I told him I hated him.

I don't want that to be the last thing I ever say to him.

Andrea Glass
Did you hear Abbie Kerr didn't come home last night?

Belinda Brown
More attention seeking.

Tracey Mullan
Hope they've checked her auntie's house lol

FORTY-TWO

 Greater Glasgow Police

Appeal for Information: Missing Teen – Port Glasgow area

The police are concerned about fourteen-year-old Abbie Kerr, who had not returned home. She was last seen on Saturday. She was wearing a dark hooded jacket and dark jeans, has black hair and blue eyes.

If anyone has information about Abbie and her whereabouts, please phone the Greenock police station.

40 💬 357 ❤ 9 💬

BanterBoy commented:

That'll be the least called number in history.

25 ❤

I can hear the rain dripping on the corrugated-iron roof high above me. At least it isn't coming in here. I seem to be in some sort of shaft. It's damp and disgusting, but the rain isn't coming in. If it's Sunday (is it still Sunday?), no one will be coming to work. Won't there be security patrols? I try shouting again, but my voice is hoarse and my throat hurts too much. The last time I ate was Saturday breakfast and I hardly had anything then. Don't want to think about that, it was the last time I saw Dad.

My head is full of thoughts and fears. The only thing that stops me panicking is trying to work out everything that's happened. Trying to make it clear in my head. So go back, Abbie. What happened next?

Why would Jude want to do this to me? It's as if she wanted to see me humiliated, broken. In despair. And I am. What day did I almost walk into the river? Seems a long time ago now. I wanted to die; I wanted it to be over.

What was the last message UNKNOWN sent? *It's almost over.* As if whoever it is was sure they'd pushed me to the edge.

Who knew I had such a fear of clowns? Everyone in my class. But Jude hadn't been there that day. Does that mean Jude isn't UNKNOWN?

There has to be a clue in something that was said, or done. I'm trying to remember. It's there and then it's gone.

Frances says she was deliberately tripped up. Her fall was not an accident. And who is the prime suspect? Me. But what had I ever done to Frances?

I find I'm crying. I can't stop crying. The least likely suspect is always the one who is guilty. And Frances is my least likely suspect. Don't let it be Frances. Please don't let it be Frances. Because hers was the only kindness I found, I so want that to be real.

---

xtraceymullanx commented:

She's still missing. Good riddance I say.

---

andreaglass15 commented:

Maybe we should have a candlelit vigil for her. I don't think

24 ♥

vanilla_kisses commented:

Don't worry. She'll come back once she's had enough publicity.

18 ♡

---

robbiegee commented:

She might not come back. I heard she was going to get expelled on Monday.

23 ♡

Princess4581 commented:

Or arrested for what she done to Frances.

31 ♡

Mon_the_Morton commented:

Nae wonder she ran away.

12 ♡

FORTY-THREE

It's light and I can hear voices. Men's voices. Someone's singing. Am I dreaming? I open my eyes. Everything's grey, but I can still hear a voice. Someone's definitely singing. Tuneless, blinking awful singing, but the sweetest sound to my ears. I try to scream. Where's my voice? What if they go away, and don't come back? Why can't I make a sound? I push myself to my feet, and try to yell. My throat feels as if it's closing up, I can't breathe. I know I'm panicking, but I am so afraid whoever is here is going to leave and I'll be alone again. Engines are starting up, drowning out any sound I might make. Already the singing is fading, the voices are going. NO. No. No. I can't let them go away now.

The sound came from deep in my soul. A scream so loud I imagined it bouncing off the grey roof, and I screamed again, and I screamed again.

Feet pounded on the ground above me. Someone shouted, "Whit's that?"

"Over here!"

And then a face. A man in a yellow helmet looked down at me, so far, yet so near.

Then I couldn't make a sound. I only held up my hand to reach out to him.

I couldn't stop crying, or shaking.

"Don't worry, we'll get you out. Abbie, isn't it?"

How did he know my name? But I didn't ask; I just wanted him to get me out.

Another face appeared, another man in a yellow helmet. "We're getting a ladder!" he shouted down to me. "How did you get down there?" I don't think he expected an answer because his face disappeared again.

The first man stayed. "Don't panic."

Was I panicking? My teeth were chattering, everything was shaking. I tried to get to my feet, but my legs melted under me and I ended up back on the ground.

"Stay where you are, I'm coming to get you."

Next thing a steel ladder slid down. The man reached the ground and held out his hand to stop me from climbing but I didn't know if I could climb anyway. I was suddenly aware that I'd been doing the toilet down there, but the man didn't seem to notice. He took my arm gently.

"One step at a time, I'll be right behind you."

I could feel his hand guiding me, protecting me as I climbed. I stood on one foot, hauled with my arms. I was getting out of there. The thought made me shake even more and I lost my footing.

"Careful, careful," he said.

And I was out! I felt like kissing them all, these big men with their yellow helmets and bright yellow jackets.

"You're lucky we heard you. We were ready to slap a steel pillar into that shaft."

The thought made me shake even more.

"Your dad's on his way," one of them said, as I was wrapped in a blanket.

"You know my dad?" My voice sounded grizzled, as if it was being forced through gravel.

"He's our union man," another man said. "He's been worried sick about you."

"You've been front-page news in the *Tele*,"

the first man said, the one who'd come down for me, but his voice didn't sound as kindly now.

I just wanted my dad.

I was given a cup of hot sweet tea in a big mug and I've never tasted anything so good in my life.

And then my dad was there; he came rushing at me. And he folded me up in his arms and I just wanted to stay there forever. "I'm sorry, Dad."

"What on earth happened, Abbie, how did you get in here?"

I started to tell him, about the texts, about the clown, but he put his hand over my mouth as if he didn't want me to say more in front of these men. "Time for that later," he whispered. Then he lifted me and carried me and I saw an ambulance waiting at the shipyard entrance. "I don't want to go to hospital, Dad," I murmured. "I just want to go home."

"They need to check you over."

So I trusted him. I must have slept, because when I opened my eyes I was in a hospital room. "I think we should keep her overnight," a doctor was saying to my dad. "She'll be fine, her foot isn't broken, but it's a bad sprain and she's dehydrated."

I began to shake again. "No, no, I just want to go home."

"Can I stay with her?" Dad asked, and the doctor said yes, and that made it a bit better. They let me have a shower, and that made me feel better too. I slipped into bed, with Dad on a chair by my side. I wanted to talk, to explain to him about the text, but as soon as I closed my eyes I was deep in sleep. Safe because Dad was close beside me.

In my dreams I'm not safe. I'm still in that dark place, trapped forever. It's my rescue that has been the dream.

I jumped awake and saw my dad, stretched out on a chair, head lolling back, snoring softly, and then I cried. I love him so much and I was so glad to be back with him by my side.

I dozed again and I heard the door open. I opened my eyes expecting to see a nurse come to check on me. But it isn't a nurse. It's the clown grinning at me round the door. And the room is suddenly in darkness. *It isn't over, Abbie.*

I scream, "Leave me alone! Leave me alone!"

Dad leaped from his chair and grabbed me in the nick of time before I could fall out of the bed. "You're having a nightmare, Abbie."

A nurse stood at the open door. She wasn't smiling.

"You've been through a terrible ordeal, Abbie," Dad comforted me. "It would give anyone nightmares."

The nurse left, still unsmiling.

"What's wrong with her?" Then it hit me that no one had smiled. And I knew why. "They think I did it on purpose, don't they? They think all this was some kind of hoax, another Abbie hoax."

"Go back to sleep, Abbie, we'll talk about it in the morning."

"But it wasn't, Dad. Honest. It wasn't."

After that, how was I supposed to sleep? They thought I did it all so I could be famous again. No one would believe I saw the clown. I hardly believed it myself by then. I had no proof. Where had my phone gone? Lost forever probably. Once again I would be known as Attention-Seeking-Abbie.

Yet in those intermittent moments between sleep and wakefulness, something came together. All the messages I had received, my dad's text, Sara Flynn, the television, and all at once the things that had been nagging at me in the dark were clear. I was sure I'd worked it out. I was sure I knew now who UNKNOWN really was.

Trouble is, I would never be able to prove it.

FORTY-FOUR

A policewoman came in next morning to talk to me. She wanted to know why I was there, at the shipyard. I hesitated so long before answering, it sounded like I was making up a lie.

"We know you've been reporting texts you say you've been getting," she said, stressing 'you say'. Which made it harder for me to speak.

Dad squeezed my arm. "Just tell the truth, Abbie."

So I did. I told her about the text I received from Dad. When I said that, her eyes moved to him.

"I never sent any text," he said.

"I thought he might be taking us out for dinner."

"We do that now and again." He was trying to back me up.

"And then what?"

"And then I..." I couldn't mention the clown. It all sounded too crazy.

"How did you end up in the shaft?"

"I thought I saw... somebody, and I went after them, and I stumbled and fell and..."

"You followed a total stranger, in the dark."

"I thought it might have been... the one sending me the texts."

"Can you identify this... person you were running after?"

She didn't believe me. I could hear it in her tone. Yeah, I thought, I can identify them. A clown with a scarlet slash for a smile. I didn't dare tell her that. So I shook my head. "No."

She put her notebook away and stood up. She motioned my dad to follow her. I heard them whispering outside the door. My dad's voice got louder.

"Have you never heard of online bullying? That's all she's been getting since this began. And nobody's listened. If my girl says she got a text from me then somehow someone sent her a text from my phone. It wouldn't be so hard – I often leave it lying about. If she says she saw someone and followed them, then I will believe her. That's what she needs right now. Someone to believe her."

Next minute, he was back in the room. His face was red. "I let you down, Abbie. Things have been happening to you and I didn't listen."

I should have been the one apologising to him. I wanted to tell him that, but all I could say was, "Can I go home, Dad?"

Turned out home wasn't the safe place I thought it would be.

Sara Flynn and her tv crew were waiting on the road. Neighbours were out too. None of them were applauding.

"Why are they here, Dad?"

"Because you were missing for THREE days. You've been rescued. Everyone's interested." He put his arm around me as we got out of the car. "Stay close and don't say a word."

Sara came running up to me. I moved closer to Dad and he shoved the camera away from my face. "Let her get inside, for goodness sake."

"We just want to know what happened, Abbie. How did you get yourself trapped? Some people are saying it was deliberate."

"Get out of here!" I could feel the anger in

my dad's voice. And there was anger in me too. Deliberate. That's what they'd all been thinking.

Sara called out, "Will there be any charges brought against Abbie?"

As soon as we were inside I turned to Dad. "What does she mean? Charges? Not more charges please."

He brushed it aside. "There won't be. Don't worry about that."

But I was worried. If they believed I did this deliberately, created a missing girl story for a second time, surely the Procurator Fiscal would charge me, or have me committed?

"What have they been saying, Dad, about me? I want to know."

He rubbed a hand across his brow. For a moment I thought he wasn't going to answer me. "Not very nice things, Abbie. No one took it seriously when you didn't come home. But they didn't know the argument we'd had."

"I really did get a text, Dad. It said you were going to pick me up at the roundabout. If I had my phone, I could show you. I must have lost it when I fell."

"I believe you," he said simply.

"I don't blame people not believing me. But someone is doing this to me. Someone who really hates me."

Dad sat me on the sofa and took a seat on the coffee table across from me, holding my hands. "I want you to forget about the past, Abbie. I want this to be a new beginning for us. You're back and you're safe and that's all I care about. I'm going to get you into a new school. Another new beginning. I just want this to be over, Abbie. For both of us."

I knew he didn't want me to go on about someone being after me, someone hating me.

I wanted a new beginning too. I had no phone, so there could be no more texts. But I couldn't leave it like this. Now I thought I knew who UNKNOWN was, I couldn't just let it go.

FORTY-FIVE

I was so glad I didn't have my phone that night. I'd seen an item on the news about my return, and it was clear there was no sympathy or worry about me. I was about to be expelled, reason enough for going, and I was under suspicion for what happened to Frances. I cried when I saw what they said about me. If I'd had my phone to read them, I knew the posts and messages would be flying, and I'd feel even worse.

So there I was, home, and nothing had really changed. If anything, things had got worse for me. But at least me and Dad were ok. He believed me, or loved me enough to pretend to.

He switched the tv off when he came into the room and saw what I was watching on the news.

"Enough. Forget about all that."

"Did everyone make it hard for you when I was

gone? Did you find it difficult getting anyone to look for me?"

He answered me with a tight smile. "We're going to put this behind us, Abbie. Move on."

The tears welled up in my eyes. I was never one for crying, yet I cry at the slightest thing now. "What if they charge me for what happened to Frances?"

"We'll fight it," he said simply.

"I didn't do it. I would never do anything like that."

He reached out to me and clasped my hand. "I know you wouldn't, Abbie. You might punch someone in the face, but you would never be so devious as to put something across the stairs to trip them."

"Unfortunately, you're the only one who thinks that."

We sat in comfortable silence for a while, then his phone pinged and I jumped. Texts do that to me.

He held the phone so I could read the message.

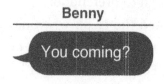

Benny

You coming?

"My pal, Benny," he explained. One of his union friends. "I was supposed to drop him off some papers. Totally forgot."

"Go then," I told him. "I'll be fine."

"You sure? I'll be back in an hour. I promise."

"I'll watch some tv."

"Not the news, ok?" He smiled. "Tell you what… I'll bring in pizza, what do you say?"

"Sounds good to me."

I heard his car drive off, and I knew he didn't want to leave me, but in a way I was glad of the time alone, safe in my own house, to think things through. I had no proof of what I suspected, and no way of getting any proof either. UNKNOWN had been too clever. The text pretending to be my dad must have come from someone who knew we'd had a fight, someone who lured me to the shipyard. Someone who had been watching my dad and knew how he left his phone lying about. Someone who could grab it quickly, send a text, then delete it.

I thought of Dad. A text from Benny. But was it Benny really? Was he being lured somewhere, or… was the text to get him to leave the house, to leave me here alone?

You're being paranoid, Abbie, I told myself.

Almost on cue the doorbell rang. I hoped it was Dad come back because he'd forgotten something or he'd changed his mind. I hobbled to the door. It must be Dad, it has to be him.

I pulled the door open.

It wasn't Dad.

FORTY-SIX

I hobbled into school on my crutches. My stomach was heaving. Could I face what was going to happen today? The school was strangely silent. Lessons had begun. I headed for the auditorium. Our first lesson on Friday was always in there. Our whole year group. All gathered together, all hating me.

I pushed open the door and was in full view of them. The teacher hadn't arrived. This teacher was never on time. I knew that. They were all chatting, talking, mostly about me. I'd heard about the tweets, messages discussing me. No one believed I'd really been missing.

Big Belinda noticed me first. I saw her nudging Andrea, who turned to look at me and opened her mouth dramatically in shock. Tracey only sniggered. Robbie stood up. Then they were all looking and

I could read their minds and their minds were filled with scorn, hate and ridicule.

I shouted and my voice rang round the auditorium. "Aye, it's me. I'm here. For the last time. D'ye know how I'm here? I'm being expelled. Are you all happy now? You're getting rid of me."

There was actually a round of applause when I said that.

"Well, I am not going on my own. Because I know who this UNKNOWN is, and now I can prove it. And then everybody will know I was the one telling the truth. Me!" My voice rose higher, more like a scream than a shout. Robbie ran down the steps and grabbed me by the shoulder. I shook him away.

"You're making a complete fool of yourself. Come on." He tried to pull me away but I yanked myself free of him.

"You all wait and see. Somebody is going to be sorry. Thought you had me, didn't you? Well, I got you!"

"You're going to get done for Frances," someone shouted.

"That wasn't me. And I can prove that as well."

I threw one of the crutches across the floor and

it clattered on the wood and slid to a halt at Belinda's feet.

"That could have killed somebody!" she yelled.

And I screamed, "I want to kill somebody. I could have been killed in that shaft! What's been done to me is killing meeeee!" My screams echoed like a wail across the auditorium.

"Got to get her out of here." Robbie waved for someone to come over and help him. It was the three witches who came, never wanting to miss the action: Tracey, Belinda and Andrea.

"We've got to get her to calm down."

I screamed again. "Calm down? After what's been done to me? I'm not the one who should calm down." I was shaking. I was actually shaking.

Andrea tried to take my arm. "Get away from me!" I screamed at her, and I hobbled from the auditorium.

Robbie was right beside me. He gripped my arm again. "You're making a fool of yourself."

"Oh you wait and see! See who's going to be the fool when I'm finished."

I heard Belinda laughing. Hard to disguise her big daft laugh.

I swung round at her. "What are you laughing at?

You're not going to be laughing when I tell the head what I know."

Robbie had to force me towards the janitor's closet. "Get in there, Abbie, calm down, please." He looked back at Andrea. "You gonny stay with her? I'm away to get a teacher. She's out of control."

"I'm not! I'm not! I'm not!" But my screaming only proved I was.

The closet had shelves, buckets and brushes, there was a small desk piled high with boxes. I backed against one of the shelves and yelled again, "I don't want them in here."

Andrea waved Tracey and Belinda away. I was glad to see them go. I didn't want everybody there. It was hard enough.

"I'm not out of control, Andrea," I told her, as she closed the door behind them. "I know you don't like me, but I'm the victim here."

There was a time when I thought she did like me. The phone call she had made, praising me for all I was doing for Jude, asking if there was anything she could do to help.

"You said you know who this UNKNOWN is?"

"I do."

"Who is it then?"

"I'm only telling the head."

"He won't believe you, Abbie. Nobody believes you."

"But they will, Andrea, when I show them the proof."

"Who is it, Abbie? Don't keep me in suspense."

And I couldn't keep from saying it any longer.

"It's Jude."

She looked totally surprised. "Jude?"

"I know, last person you suspect, eh? She fooled everybody, but I've had a lot of time to think about it, and it's so clear to me. She made it look as if I was the one behind the plan and everybody believed that, because wee Jude's too stupid to come up with a clever plan like this. Isn't that what everybody says? And her staying at my auntie's…? Jude would never have thought of that. So that must have been me as well. Do you see what she was doing, Andrea? Fooling us all. But I'm telling you, Andrea, Jude is smarter than any of us."

"Jude?" she said again.

"I know, I know, it took me a long time, such a long time to figure it out. I blamed everybody else, I kept dismissing her, but when you really think about it, it's the only explanation."

"Well, I suppose, if you say so..." Her voice drifted off.

"Andrea, you were taken in too. And you don't believe it because you like her. But you know it was you that started all this."

"Me!" she straightened, moved back, but I pulled her towards me.

"You dumped her, remember? She was heartbroken. I found her and she was crying her eyes out, and I told her..." I stopped. What I had told Jude had been pretty insulting to Andrea. "Never mind what I told her, but I was trying to help her. I gave her good advice and she starts phoning me and thanking me, and then she says, 'I've got a great idea.'" My voice was breaking but I had to go on. "I should never have listened to her, it just seemed to be such a good plan, a clever plan. But of course the clever bit was not coming back when she said she would. So I'm left getting all the flack, and then she does come back – in full view of the cameras. Class, Andrea, pure class. You and me could never come up with anything like that. We're just not in her league."

"Nobody's going to believe it was Jude, Abbie. Everybody knows she's thick as a brick."

I shook my head. "That's what she wants people to think, Andrea. But, no offence, Andrea, when it comes to Jude, you're the one that's thick as a brick."

Andrea stifled a giggle with her hand. "Me? Thick as a brick? Jude Tremayne cleverer than me?"

"Hard to believe I know, but it's true... and I've got the proof."

"Proof? What proof?"

"I've got a photo on my phone of Jude pushing me down that shaft."

She looked really puzzled. "You've got your phone? A photo of her?" Then she smiled. "But I mean... how are you going to prove that's Jude? A photo of a clown?"

And I stepped back before I said, "What makes you think it was a photo of a clown, Andrea?"

FORTY-SEVEN

Andrea took a deep breath. "You said it was a clown chasing you."

I shook my head. "No, I never mentioned a clown near the shaft, Andrea. I knew nobody would believe me. So how did you know?"

You can see a face changing, from an innocent schoolgirl to something menacing. And that's what I saw in that moment. Andrea's whole expression changed.

I asked again, "How did you know, Andrea? Did Jude make you do it, Andrea? Did she trick you the way she tricked me? Because we can both go to the head and tell him."

"What? Jude Tremayne trick me? Make *me* do something? Nobody makes me do anything I don't want to do. It was never Jude, Abbie. It was always me."

I shook my head. "No. You're not clever enough for this."

And that got her, as I knew – hoped – it would. She snapped at me. "Me? Not clever enough for this? Clever enough to be in the toilets that day when wimpy Jude is crying all over the sinks. You didn't know that, did you? I heard everything. You called *me* a loser? You? No-mates-Abbie calling me a loser! Me... You said you'd never let anybody, especially somebody like me, get to you – nothing would break you. That's when I came up with *my* plan, Abbie Kerr. Mine! I would see you go down and down, till you could go no further. I would break you. We'd see who was a 'strong person'. Jude was up for it – she'd be up for anything if I promised to be her 'friend forever'. You were the one I thought would be hard to convince, but no, I got Jude to ask, and you were up for it too. I got a copy of your auntie's keys one day when you left your bag lying around. Dead easy. I was the one told Jude to stay where she was that night of the vigil. I even told her exactly when to come back. I knew the tv was on her doorstep, but a real bit of luck you were there as well."

"And UNKNOWN? You've been UNKNOWN all along?"

"Dead easy to send a message from a withheld number. You know I'm good at I.T., Abbie. Just as easy to lift your dad's phone for ten minutes and send you a text."

"Were Tracey and Belinda in on it too?"

She laughed outright. "Them two? They're thicker than Jude. No, Jude was the only one, and she had nothing to do with the texts. Apart from the ones in the supermarket." She had such a cruel smile. "Didn't spot her there, did you? She saw you with the chicken, and then she bolted and messaged me." She folded her arms and stared at me, smug written all over her face. "Finding out you were so scared of clowns was the icing on the cake."

"And you got into my garden just to frighten me?"

"You should have seen your face. I thought you were going to faint."

"And you lured me to the shipyard?"

"Remember Jude was on the phone when you arrived that day? Who do you think she was talking to? I heard you telling her you'd fallen out with your dad. It was perfect."

"You saw me falling down that shaft, Andrea. I could have died down there. You didn't know if I'd

270

broken my ankle or my neck. And they were getting ready to hammer a steel pillar into that shaft. If I'd been unconscious..." I shuddered. How could she do such a thing?

She waved it aside. "So? You'd be no loss to anybody. I told a few folk that you'd run away cause you wanted more attention. A wee whisper here, a wee whisper there. So easy. Everybody in this school's thick."

"Why... why are you telling me all this, Andrea? I'm going to Mr Barr."

That only made her laugh. "Oh Abbie, who is ever going to believe a word you say?"

The door opened.

It was Robbie. "Just about everybody, Andrea. Come and see."

Andrea followed him out, still talking. "She's definitely lost it, Robbie, you should hear the things..." and then she stopped. There was her face, up on the big screen in the atrium, and she was confessing everything. "What? What's happening?"

I came out behind her. "Smile, Andrea, you've just been framed."

FORTY-EIGHT

Andrea's confession was played over and over on every screen in the school. Our whole year group had seen it live in the auditorium. People had to grab Tracey and Belinda to stop them from going after Andrea. "Thick as bricks are we?"

I would have let them at her.

But I had got UNKNOWN at last.

And who did I owe it to? It was all thanks to Robbie.

He was the one at the door that night when Dad went to Benny's.

"Hi Abbie," he had said. "I've got something that belongs to you." And he'd held out my phone.

For a second I thought he was UNKNOWN, but only for a second. Because then he'd smiled and said, "Proves everything you said was true, Abbie. You did get a text from your dad, and there was a clown."

I still couldn't take it in. "How did you get that?"

He grinned. "I went back to the scene of the crime. Took a bit of finding – it was sunk right in the mud. But there it was. And once I'd cleaned it up and recharged it, I could turn it on."

"But why... why did you go back?"

"Because when they started saying it was you that made Frances trip, even I struggled to believe that. You drive people potty, but I didn't think you would set a trap like that, and I began to think... if you didn't do that, maybe you didn't do any of the other things."

"My hero," I said.

"Don't be sarcastic. Anyway, after you were rescued, everybody heard about the text you said you'd got, and how your phone was missing, and how handy that was for you. And I thought, what if she is telling the truth, and she really did lose her phone when she fell?"

"I could kiss you, Robbie."

He took a step back. "Please don't. I've not got the antidote."

That made me laugh. "I know who sent that text. Robbie, I think I know who has been behind this all along."

Because I had been figuring out something else.

It was what had been niggling at me when I was trapped in the shaft. That text I got from Dad.

Meet me at 5 at Ferguzons shipyard. Made me remember another text I'd seen from Andrea. *My bestezt friend.* She had that little habit of putting a 'z' instead of an 's'.

The answer's on the television, Sara Flynn had said in my dream. That kept coming back to me. She was right. I remembered the piece I'd seen about folie á deux. Two people who, when they get together, can do evil things. Of course it couldn't just be Jude; Jude wasn't clever enough or bad enough to come up with such a plan. But someone else was, and who else but Andrea? Andrea, so proud of her own I.T. skills, Andrea, who knew how desperate Jude was to be her friend again, so desperate she would agree to anything.

And when I thought about it like that, it all came together.

But how to prove it?

It was Robbie who had come up with the idea of tricking her. "Saw it in an old episode of 'Criminal Minds'" he had told me. "It's called 'reverse psychology'. If you tell her she wasn't clever enough to come up with this but Jude was, if you keep on and on about it, Andrea won't be able to take that. She'll break. And we'll record it all."

He said he'd set up tiny cameras from the studio in the janitor's closet, disguise them, and our whole conversation would be fed live through the school. It sounded so simple when he said it, but I was shaking all over that day. What would I have done if it hadn't worked? I don't know. I didn't think that far ahead. It had to work.

EPILOGUE

Andrea left the school. She was charged and shamed. Her confession, caught on camera, went viral on YouTube. (Well, she always wanted to be famous.) Now she was the one discussed on tv. 'Folie á deux' now referred to Andrea and Jude. Jude broke like an egg as soon as she was questioned. Confessed everything, blamed Andrea. Somehow I don't think that particular 'friends forever' duo will last.

Andrea had more than just a cruel streak. The police psychologists said there was something really wrong with her.

I still have nightmares about being down in that shaft. What if I hadn't been found? What if I'd been an unsolved mystery?

I shake the thought of that away. Didn't happen.

And so, what did happen to me? Do you think I am now the most popular girl in the school? Ha! No way, that title belongs deservedly to Frances, the only one through all of this who was kind to me. Nice to everyone. Good people do exist. They're everywhere.

I enjoy school. I still argue all the time with Robbie, but I kind of like that. Josh Creen will never forgive me; he still glares at me in the corridor, and I can't really blame him.

But I wasn't going crazy, I wasn't mad. I was so close to madness it scared me. It made me realise how people can manipulate you and play with your mind. That was what Andrea had done. She had spread so much evil with her wicked whispers.

I don't use my phone so much now. I turn it off at home, and talk to my dad. At night, I put it in my bedside drawer. And when I go out with friends (me, with friends!), it stays in my bag.

I still feel a chill when I hear the ping saying I have a new message. My first thought is always, A message from who? And I hold my breath before I look, and pray: as long as it isn't from UNKNOWN...

Share a selfie
to spread the lie
and we'll share a secret.

#SecretsRumoursLies